Annie's Enviable Position

Jordan Muncz

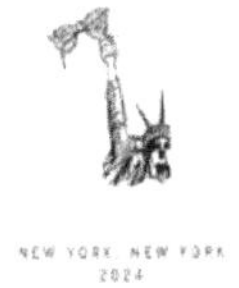

The Shortsighted New Yorker
New York, NY 10009

ISBN: 979-8-9907940-1-6

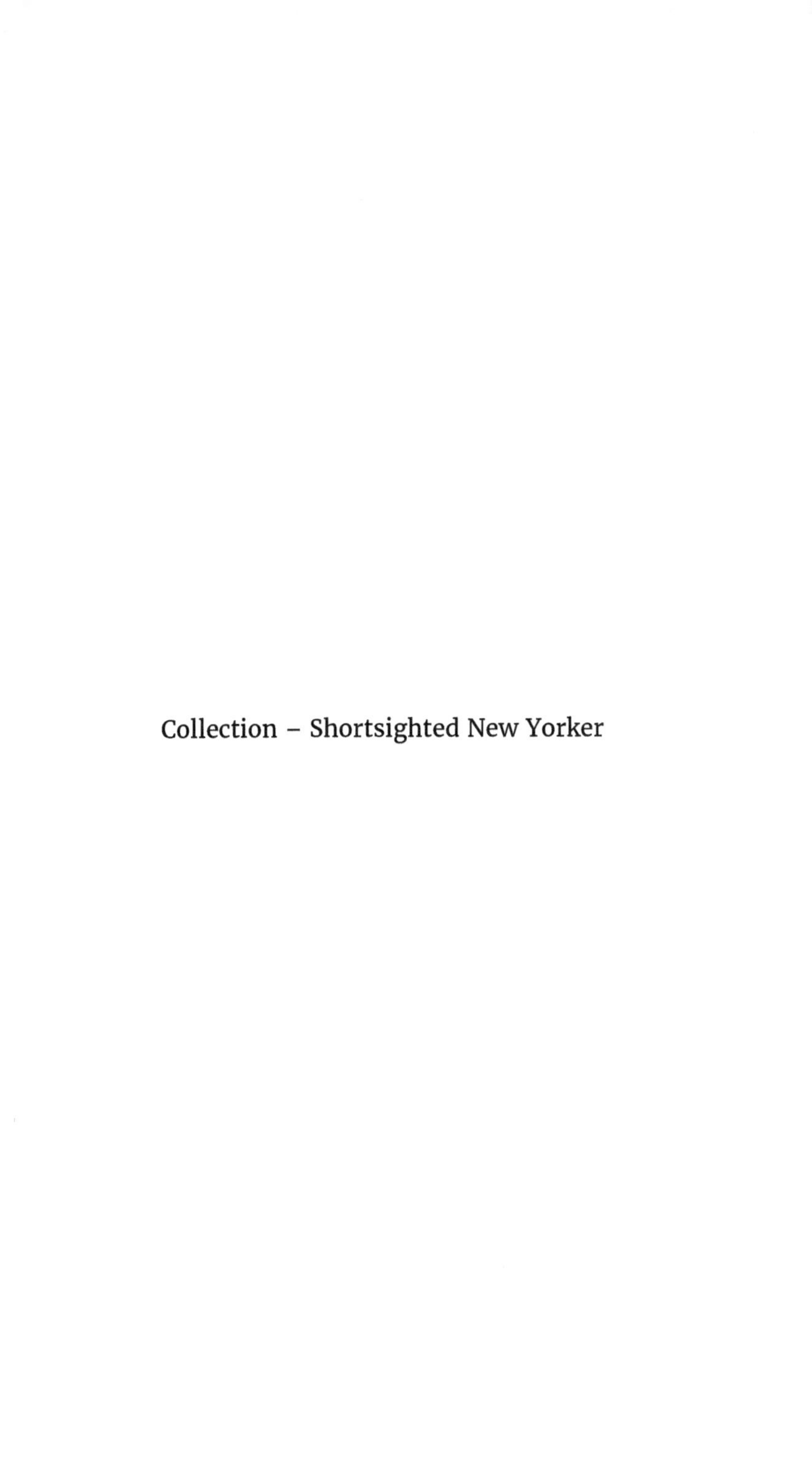

Collection – Shortsighted New Yorker

CONTENTS

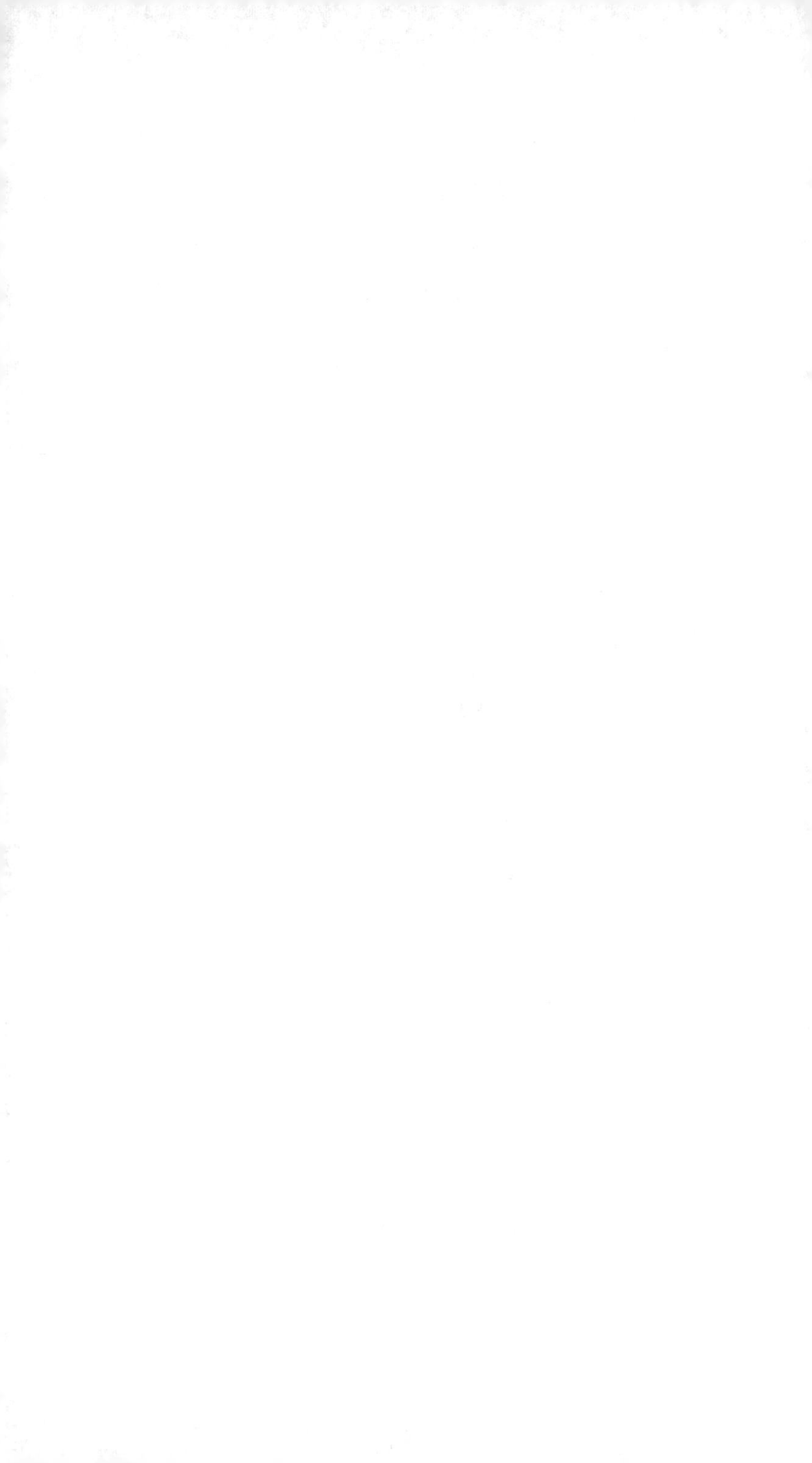

ACKNOWLEDGMENTS

Jordan Muncz would like to thank everyone of you, and especially the Shelleys, Pierce and Mary.

1 FOREWORD

Imperceptible imperfection, harder to describe than to see, makes him lean closer to the mirror. His bare feet expose strong veins and even stronger, immaculate toes. His leotards add modesty to a marble-like body. A make-up brush in his right hand, for a moment he seems unsure whether the flaw has been imagined.

"M. Nijinsky" is heard from outside his door. Whispers, silence, and finally a large bouquet of roses make it into his room carried by a humorless, surprisingly well- scrubbed ruffian. Save the flowers, there is no other indication of the beautiful spring evening; M. Nijinsky's rehearsal suite is in the basement of the Châtelet Theater.

The momentary distraction discarded, the dancer concentrates on his reflection. Displeased, perhaps, he moves to the sink and starts washing off the unfinished makeup. His mechanical moves become faster and more determined as if some impurity is hard to reach. Finally, the water splash ceases. The sought result must have been reached. His eyes turn murky. The help materializes behind. Nijinsky stands up and fusses while being draped with a thick Turkish towel.

"Vatsa, please, stand still," the towering Russian moujik turned domestic servant addresses the dancer paternally. Nijinsky smiles, vaguely pleased, obeys, and when all is done, moves back to the make- up table. Meticulously he replaces layers of himself with layers of the slave he will soon dance in the ballet "Le Pavillon d'Armide." Suddenly, a light tap at the door awakes him alert from a mountain of talc powder.

"Vasilly," the guest addresses the domestic who, politely bowing, lets him in, then takes the coat and fedora from his gloved hands. Nijinsky does not turn to see him, but smiles at the mirror which inadvertently reflects his greeting.

"Sasha, I don't want you here," Nijinsky finally says.

With graceful moves, unexpected for such a heavy-set bloke further handicapped by the three-piece tight suit, and a strong sense of entitlement, Serghey Petrovich Diaghileff, Sasha, bends and leans his head on Vatsa's shoulder. Sasha is the king of the Russian Ballets presented abroad as "Ballets Russes," and seldom indulges in emotional behavior.

Through a space loop, as if it were a magnifying glass, Annie watches this scene unfold from her mother's apartment. Vio, one of her nicknames, lives on Blvd. St. Michel, when in Paris. Beckoned to visit, Annie finally accepted, and time travelled all the way from New York 2016 to Paris 1909. A dhampire, only one step below vampires, Annie does not know jetlag. Like a soccer fan she's ready to stand and cheer whatever events her mom, the vampire vigilante, happens to scrutinize.

"Bite," Annie encourages Sasha, sitting on the edge of a soft cushion. Each time she visits Paris, Vio's routine enwraps her with excitement. Vio's job is to keep the Russian dhampir emigration in check, and especially to impede Russian dancers from becoming a dhampir cover-up or fodder. Sasha, the second generation Russian dhampir, a humiliation to the vampire tribe, half human and half vampire, is the main villain in her mom's surveillance. He spends his time and deadly bites on Vatsa Nijinsky, the 20th century ballet legend, and the rest of it, he bullies, threatens, and entices "mules" to work for him.

The image of the perfect dilettante, Vio pretends to be interested in taking private lessons with Sasha's ballet maestro, Cheketti, in exchange for providing the Ballets Russes with unlimited soirees and summer retreats. Her centennial has made her wise, preserved her killing skills, while sparing her wrinkles, tooth decay, or arthritis. Sasha seems unsuspecting.

In the basement of the theater, Sasha is absorbed by Vatsa's robust, youthful, neck.

"The bite," Annie stands up ready to clap.

"One of the many Sasha bestowed on his protégé," Vio adds. In time, Sasha submits Vatsa to a long process of contamination. Each bite infects his protégé with just enough destruction to keep him going while he's still of interest to Sasha.

'Vatsa puts up no resistance. Pleased with his pupil's reaction, Sasha rewards him with tenderness. He brushes away a lock of hair from the dancer's face. Vatsa closes his lids in appreciation. Then, as if in a trance, he mimics the move. In his hand, Sasha's gesture becomes a youth's desire to observe the world more clearly, only he does not. Not anymore. With each dhampir bite, Vatsa becomes depleted of will, a marionette in Sasha's hands.

Vio fiddles with a red gardenia. She puts it in Annie's coral, or "carrot-like," as Miriam loves to add, hair. The colors clash. Shaking her head in dislike she moves it down to Annie's boutonniere.

"Mom," Annie brushes her away. "Stop fidgeting. I cannot see."

"The child is taking notes, Vio. Bravo," Miriam's voice makes itself heard.

Ignoring her mom's audible presence, Vio appraises

Annie's look, and pleased, gets up to stretch and smoke. In her sumptuous white silk, multi-layered outfit, a rich contrast with her white, flawless skin and dark wavy hair, Vio moves with purpose and youthfulness. No one would doubt her Parisian identity as Princess Edmond de Polignac, the superb equestrian, and Grand Dame of the arts. Money is well spent in her petite, freshly manicured hands.

Vio's departure moves the space loop along, and Annie has no power to open her own. Surveilling Sasha is neither her assignment, nor her memory, so Annie finds herself soon hassled to get out of the servants' way. Ignorant of Annie's enviable position as Vio's daughter – Annie's clothes do not indicate any such connection – they get busy with the preparations for the soiree pushing her aside. Still, despite their fashion dissonance, and their different skin and hair color, the mother-daughter resemblance is noticeable – they are both driven by forces beyond their control.

As soon as Diaghileff leaves the dressing suite, elegantly wiping off a sliver of blood from his mustache, the muscle man re-appears and dresses the dancer in his costume. Vatsa, in a visible trance, is still and obliging. The first layer of costume is a white, yellow and silver outfit embellished with festoons of silk, lace, ruffles and ermine. Next is an ornate, heavy top-coat, and wired skirt. Finally, come the knee- breeches with garters. With each layer Vatsa evolves. He is no longer the somewhat awkward petit man with disproportionate muscles and feline shaped eyes. When the jeweled choker sits around his neck, he has metamorphosed into an object of sexual desire. With the addition of the white silk turban with an ostrich-feather he ceases being Vatsa. He is Nijinsky, Sasha's Favorite Slave. For now.

In her Princess Edmond de Polignac's pied-à-terre, Vio's preparations for the after- the-show party have come to fruition. The servants' chase finished, Annie searches for a place to hide, when she believes she hears her grandmother's scolding voice echoing

from behind the grave amid bottles of champagne and bowls of ice for the caviar. Annie wonders but quickly stops tripping over a ladder: a young man in overalls hangs up a large portrait of Vatsa in a bathing suit. She frowns losing her balance, puzzled.

"We are in 1909, correct?" Vio nods approvingly. "So, what is this Bakst 1910 painting doing here?" Annie asks with a perfunctory thank-you smile for the help: the young man stabilized her unsteadiness.

"I did this."

"You paint?"

"When I cannot sleep. Waiting for a mortal to fall in love with, for a little while." Annie instinctively leans back away from her mother. "Annie, don't be silly." Annie accepts a coupe of champagne, and sips. She still does not like it. She returns it to the help. "Bakst will ask to borrow it for his own portrait of Vatsa – who by next year, in 1910, won't be able to pose staying still."

"Mom, this is a remarkable work of art."

"Prince Myshkin likes it, too."

"Myshkin?"

"I like Bakst's painting better." Vio smokes pensively in front of the unsigned portrait, ignoring the question. "Any way, there is no similarity between the two."

"Save the bandana covering his left ear." Annie adds watching her mother's youthful hand betraying no age taking hold of another flute of Champagne. So lucky that alcohol has no effect on dhampires, she thinks.

"It's the first proof of the bite," Vio smiles pleased with her daughter's knowledge.

"Mom, who is Myshkin?" Vio looks away intensely. Opening a hollow time loop in an attempt to get help from her own mom, Miriam.

"Mom, please, you said that Myshkin likes it too."

"She meant Lev," Miriam makes her voice heard through

the time loop Vio opened for her.

"Mom, you asked Grandma Miriam to come and help you?"

"This is the most mother-daughter Kodak moment I have ever witnessed." No one reacts to her strange remark. "You remember the TV ads, don't you?" Breaking again the silence, Miriam whistles the music. Annie laughs. "Kiddo, you were your mom's stellar student."

"Briefly in elementary school. But, why are you bringing that up?"

"That god-forgotten place, Podunk, in dhampir heaven, Romania, was as boring as Radeş. Only you were too young to have your own Nicholas so you must have had books."

"I don't follow."

"Don't get snappy kiddo. You read a lot, didn't you?"

"Grandma, I did not read Dostoyevsky in elementary school, if this is what you are alluding to."

"With your gift and talent, I imagined you might have. Obviously I was wrong."

With a Chinese antique fan, Vio pushes away the smoke from Annie's eyes, but mostly her mother's voice. Irritated by the turn the conversation has taken, Annie goes through the French window onto the terrace. Red roses and gardenias, Vatsa's favorite flowers, lie everywhere. A couple of chaise lounges beckon her to relax. The sun has not yet set. The roofs of Paris look on fire. Vio is not following her. The receiver in her hand, she checks if her new toy, an Alexander Graham Bell-created telephone, works.

"Mom," Annie turns towards Vio, "please talk to me."

"Not now, darling. Not now." "Please, mom. What is going on?" "It's a long story." Vio hangs up.

"It's too early to show up in my University office. People may start talking that I'm a vampire, and you know I don't like encouraging false rumors."

"Who is Myshkin for you?" Vio finally sits down, opens her surveillance loop, lights an elegant cigarette and faces

Annie.

"Only my most favorite Dostoyevsky character, Prince Lyov Nikolaevich Myshkin."

"Lyov, I've always admired your ease for languages."

"Mom, please, don't digress."

"Every time I pronounce that name, it melts in my mouth like a soft caramel covered in rich dark chocolate."

"Mom!"

"Sorry. Imagine Russia at the end of the 19th century. Its vast land was populated with moujiks and moujik-blood-sucking..." Vio sounds like a recording.

"Aristocracy. Mom, you are telling me about Russian aristocracy? Are you going to hide behind some teaching moment? Why would you care about Prince Lyov Nikolaevich Myshkin?"

"His name melts in my mouth." Vio sounds lost in a reverie.

"If only his name..." Miriam's voice can be heard. Again.

"He is a Russian aristocrat."

"A moujik-blood sucking aristocrat, that's your storyline?" Annie stands up and opens her own time loop. She's ready to step in and leave. In a few days her time as Columbia University's writer in residence will end, and her book "The Role of Vampires in Human History," is far from finished. Vio gasps behind, but does not stop her. At the last moment Annie turns and asks. "How do you know him, mom? Dostoyevsky is not your cup of tea."

"When Sasha became my assignment, the Prince's name came across. He's funded the Ballets Russes from their inception in St. Petersburg. I was intrigued and made sure we met."

"I have never heard of a dhampir benefactor, ever actually,"

"…and lover." Miriam stops Annie in mid-sentence.

"I would not go that far." Vio demurs. "Maybe bed companion. Infrequently."

"… to get a pass from you, mom." Annie finally finishes her sentence. "Your job is to contain the dhampir phenomenon

not its patronage." She persists, "Mom, what is your interest in this man?"

"He is not a man technically."

"Vio, don't tell me homosexuality, or pederasty, disqualifies him now."

"No, mom, I am not bigoted. I was just technical."

"Is he impotent?"

"Oh, no. Au contraire!" Annie cannot take this female banter between Vio and Miriam. She regrets coming to visit her mom. It always ends on an unpleasant note with Miriam interfering from beyond the grave. "Annie, I can hear your thoughts. Wait, please. Lev used to be a man, a mere human, but now he's more. He told me Sasha had infected him by the time Dostoyevsky immortalized him as Prince Myshkin, and that is why he was depicted with epileptic-like seizures. Now, after I spent half-a-century with him, I don't know exactly what he is anymore."

"Mom, obviously he is not a man anymore. Grandpa Nicholas, and Vatsa too, died within decades, while suffering of the seizures. Despite your unending 1909-time loop how can an 1800s character still be alive in the 21st century?"

"Oh, Annie," Vio sounds exhausted, and sits down. "Do you have to get this technical?"

"Mom, we are immortal because we were vampires infected with dhampir blood, that why we are dhampires," and addressing an invisible Miriam, Annie adds, "I am not talking about suicidal dhampires, grandma."

"Keep it simple, darling. We are and remain vampires."

"Incorrect mom. We are vampire servants, dhampires, for lack of a better word. You a vigilante, making sure the Russian dhampir phenomenon remains an eastern European spectacle, and I am assigned to be a scribe spreading vampire propaganda."

"Ouch," Miriam says with a laugh. "Girls, your life sounds like a success story."

"At least we have one." Annie is on a roll. "Actually, how come you never received any assignments, grandma?" Miriam's voice is silent. "Am I wrong? Had you also received vigilante training, but kept it secret from us?" The indistinct ring of a telephone interrupts Annie. Miriam remains silent.

"Annie," Vio injects. "True, the dhampir blood brought us down a notch, and vampire skin-heads would call us dhampires."

"Mom, we have also lost the ability of traveling through time and space at will."

"Annie, we can procreate with vampires as well, and we can still answer memory calls, assignments, and … family invitations."

"That's what we know so far."

"Kiddo, and all this luggage can be avoided unless we taste a sip of our own blood."

"As the human Bible says, 'blessed are the ignorant.' "

"I have problems with that quote, as I doubt the fact that blood tasting is the only route to access knowledge. But, I agree that once you understand your enviable position, you cannot get back. It becomes a curse." Annie whines while Vio is distracted by something else. Her gaze fixates on the end of the space loop connecting her apartment to the Châtelet Theater.

Vio instinctively touches her belt. Aside from a muscular, lean body, the multi- layers of silk cover a small dagger with a gold handle.

The stage is briefly empty. Neither Armida, played by Vera Karalli, the Vicomte de Beaugency, played by Mikhail Mordkin, nor the Slave played by Nijinsky are around. Then, two dancers exit in a rush, and Nijinsky comes from the wings. He rises into an extended parabola which takes him from the wings into the stage, in all his splendor.

"He flies," Annie exclaims briefly forgetting her own torment.

"He does, but no one will call it by that name. Everybody will conspire to explain how the structure of his muscles and his toe-landing technique make the jumps visually akin to flying." Vio watches the stage carefully to spot any detail difference betraying a nefarious change, such as an extra, or a new set designer assistant.

"Mom, how can you ignore the ballet?"

"In such moments of inattention, Diaghileff receives his gift'," she whispers, "an acolyte dhampir or an infested human I have to reckon with often hides in a costume or sets crate."

"Who's the mule?"

"Mule? I like the name. I will tell Lev what you called him." Vio lets her guard down and regrets it.

"Myshkin? The human Sasha bit?" Vio is taken aback by her slip of the tongue. "Infected humans cannot time travel. Some become depraved creatures contagious and dangerous to other humans, unable to contain their destructive desires. Others become despondent, and I mean Grandpa Nicholas, or alcoholic, Daddy Tifaru. Nothing more, correct?" After a brief moment, she adds, "Oh, I almost forgot Vatsa, a genius, of sorts."

"Oh, Annie. You make it sound so clear and simple. But it's complicated. Love complicates everything," Vio has time to add.

"Knowledge cures everything, mom," "Ask your grandmother."

The phone rings again piercing through the time loop the three generations of dhampires have created with their fleeting reunion on Vio's terrace: New York, Paris and eternity beyond the grave of Radeş, a small village in Romania. The third ring comes through as the ovation in the Palace Châtelet explodes. Nijinsky has launched his legend.

From his balcony seat, Diaghileff takes all this success in. The seat next to his is occupied by a pale looking companion. His thick crop of strawberry blond hair gives him a young appearance. He whispers congratulatory nonsense. Diaghileff looks pleased. He stands up ready to bow. The companion turns. His blue eyes lost behind his horn-rimmed glasses a moment ago focus on Annie through Vio's time loop.

"It's the phone in my office." Annie announces distracted, missing the intruding stare.

"Annie, it's a memory call. You don't need to take it," Vio attempts to grab Annie, but she's gone.

"The memory manure stuck on her shoes and it stinks. To you," Miriam explains.

"Do we need to watch over her?"

"Maybe."

"How can I help my child, mom?"

"It's her memory call and she chose to answer it."

"Mom, what have I done?"

"By giving her birth? I advised you against it."

"Mom," Vio retorts as the curtain at Le Chalet falls down. Sasha's back stage. Vatsa runs past him feverish. Sasha nods towards the troupe's doctor, who follows Vatsa shortly.

"Overcome by success," Sasha tells the dancers, his earlier companion nowhere in sight.

***

2 THE PAST ALWAYS CALLS TWICE

"Privacy. Sweet privacy," Annie whispers closing the blinds to her office. Her time loop, still open, makes her visible to Princess Edmond de Polignac and her unexpected visitor. Lost staring into nothingness she finally remembers why she's back. The blinking red light.

Annie stretches her hand to grab the receiver, when an icy drift directs her gaze to the wide-open door. The cleaning crew must have left in a hurry. Cold air cramps in. Hurrying to shut the door, she slips on a copy of Strunk's Elements of Style. Squatting effortlessly, she picks it up. Rushed, her hair flying behind messes up her impeccable teen-like appearance draped in black linen pants, boyfriend cut, a soft cotton shirt topped with a linen jacket. She places the booklet neatly on the third shelf of her floor- to-ceiling bookcase, and closes the door. Ready to confront the message, some smell hurts her small nostrils and unexpectedly derails her actions. She cannot pinpoint the cause. Maybe it is the gardenia her mother put on one of her boutonnieres. She takes it away and throws it at the other end of the room. The smell persists. She picks it up and goes out in the hallway to find a garbage bin far enough.

The hallway is cooler than her office. She cannot stand the chill. Its AC wastefulness more than its artificiality. It's only May. She rushes back and closes the door behind. To no avail. The chill has followed her, only thicker. So thick that she loses control and falls in her chair.

She's stiff with expectation for the discomfort to pass. Closing her eyes undressed bodies diving down the shoot of her native Podunk morgue fill her void. An adolescent Dan, draped in a white coat, stands behind his father, the morgue director, inventorying every single one. He calls aloud, simply, "Dad, another one," and scribbles something down on a notepad.

"She has her vision," Miriam unadvisedly opens her time loop from Radeş to Paris. On his lap, Vio's mouth is constantly busy with champagne, smoke, and words, whispered in his small ear below the horn-rimmed glasses. His thin lips, earlier compressed into an impudent, ironic – almost malicious – smile, are now curled into confusion. "That fall in the freshly dug grave on top of the coffin, above Tifaru's dead mother could have been avoided." Vio lightly coughs, acknowledging to her mother the stickiness of her circumstances.

"I will bring you a glass of water," he says gently putting Vio in the chair to his left, and stands up in search for a glass. Despite his visible strength, his death-like pallor gives him an indescribably emaciated appearance. People flee when he approaches them. Only Sasha welcomes his presence, nodding encouragingly to approach him and Vatsa.

"Lev, I did not know you and Princess de Polignac were such close friends. Shall I be jealous?" He smiles without much else.

"Vio," Miriam beckons at Vio's attention. Rushing outside on the terrace, Vio accepts the time loop connection with Radeş and from there, New York. They both witness Annie's vision: Young, beautifully chiseled corpses drop down the Podunk morgue shoot. When they reach Annie's eye- level, they exit and disappear into the surrounding abyss. One corpse lingers and makes eye contact with Annie. He opens his dark almond shaped eyes and slowly fixates hers.

"Dan's!" Vio exclaims. "How is it possible?"

"Excuse me," Lev hands her the glass of water. Taking it, Vio looks at him for the first time smilelessly.

Cathartically, Annie opens her eyes, ends her hallucination, and gasps for air. She jumps up to let the horrid image drain out faster. In a trance, she picks up the receiver. The smell encircles her. She looks down and gets it. It's the leather. Her seat emanates new leather smell. During the night, her chair was changed. Her chair. She cannot stand it. The smell. The intrusion. She opens the blinds, the window, and lets the outside spring storm assault her. Neither sunlight nor water bother dhampires like her. Safe, she plays the message.

"Annie, hi, this is Dan. I called you when we were in New York City. ..Uh, about 10 days ago…Then, I called you from Canada…I thought you were on vacation or something…Uh, I wanted to talk to you. I'll call your cell tomorrow." Some background noise, then the strident click sums up everything Dan has to offer. The receiver becomes heavy in her hand. She hangs up. Then she plays it again. Then again.

"What is she doing?"

Annie plays back only the last few seconds.

"What are you doing?" Vio makes herself visible. "We both know Dan never calls back women of any consequence to him," she adds in an attempt to ease her daughter's excruciating pain.

"I've never been a mere woman, mom." Annie opens her small refrigerator and grabs a bottle of Perrier. She's thirsty. Unusually so. "Why Podunk, Romania, mom? Why did you have to bring me there?"

"Podunk was secluded from both vampires and dhampires."

"You did not want to mingle with our kind, the vampires of the east?"

"Vio, I never knew you chose to deliver your bastard vampire, sorry Annie, that would be you, in pervert dhampir country. I thought your vampire employers sent you there." Miriam resonates from everywhere.

"That's not a secret, mom, that I was sent to Podunk. I was also relieved. And 'Annie Tifaru' is not a bastard, as her patronymic indicates."

"Dhampirs love infesting both dhampires and humans. They are perverted being. All of them." Miriam repeats.

"Grandma, aren't you tired of spitting out bigoted nonsense?" And focusing on Vio, Annie adds, "So, you trusted the dhampirs whose blood tainted us into dhampires, or as you call us, vampires of the east, more than your employers, mom. Bravo!"

Silence follows Annie's tirade.

"Sorry to break it to you, kiddo, but there are no vampires of the east, as there is no Paris of the east." Miriam's voice is finally heard. "We are what we are, and there is no need to fudge the truth."

Annie laughs giving her grandma the comic relief she has probably sought all this time.

"Agreed, grandma. We are only vampire minions so eager to please that we never rebel."

"Annie, I don't find any of this funny. When the Council assigned me to Paris it rewarded my work in Podunk. Without Podunk, there would have been no Paris."

"No childless, eternally partying princess?" Annie is out of breath. "You've kept vampires safe from some imagined dhampir invasion, locking yourself up into a Mobius time loop, so your imaginary friend Ivan the Terrible, or whatever his name is, can be stopped from smuggling in infested humans. You could have killed him and stopped the carnage. You could have saved me, your own daughter, mother."

"Annie, motherhood is not that simple."

"Nothing is simple with you, mom. By the way, care to share with me what is motherhood for you? Sharing secrets and an enviable position, a country club membership, rather than a strong emotional connection?"

"You are unnecessarily harsh. When I graduated from

our Formative Years, as you might remember your own graduation, Annie, you could choose an assignment or you were given one."

"Are we going to talk about job prospects?"

"We are. We both work for a living."

"Kido, your mom was the best vampire vigilante. You may think that Podunk disappointed the soviet intellectual with its architecture, or better said, its lack of architecture, within the first minutes upon exiting the train station. But, it was an important crossroad point back when there was a USSR. Soviet dhampirs were quite inventive and reckless in their attempts to go west in vampire country. Podunk, unlike small villages like Radeş, had cheap and clean prostitutes, barely out of high school. Dhampirs loved that. Vio made sure the revelry kept going."

"Your humorous explanation in the face of adversity is amazing, grandma."

"Annie, let's give it a rest. I was happy to be the vigilante leader in a dhampir haven, and stop the spread of infested masses all over Europe. I devised the plan to contain both the dhampir and infected human threat from expanding westward."

"Mom, shall I start applauding you? You were a mere elementary school teacher with a knack for volunteer work and ignoring your offspring."

"I contained Gigi, a dhampir whom even his ally, the Soviet Party, had also identified as a threat. I came up with the one-lover verdict. I approved of Tifaru, one of his most untalented students and watched over their interaction."

Annie stops her mom. "Gigi & Tifaru, so jolly and unassuming, were your target. I am impressed."

"Gigi's cover was that of a University professor, and a high-ranking informer in the Party. When he got bored with a student he made sure the Party received an anonymous tip. The undesirable lover disappeared with no questions asked."

"First infested and then discarded his pray. That's the perfect bureaucrat story. And I thought you were a mere elementary school teacher."

"Indeed, once I became Violet, Vio for friends of all stripes."

"Kiddo, you should be proud of your mom. She was the best vigilante the vampires ever got. A busy, workaholic teacher by day, she filled her afternoons with volunteer work."

Annie remembers all too well the side effect of her mother's excellence. As a child, she experienced a growing fear of "home" – she learned how to loath and desire the privacy of their one-bedroom apartment.

"Mom, I'm home" rarely received a warm welcome. Instead, illegibly hand- written notes would lie on the kitchen table announcing that Vio, always the volunteer, had to run out for a chorus rehearsal or to arrange for a political leader's visit to the local orphanage, or most of the time just to pay a quick call with the family of a truant or missing student. "Did you know how much your absence traumatized me?" Annie confronts Vio.

Too late. Vio has returned to her hostess duty, including eavesdropping on a private conversation between Diaghileff and Vatsa, and puts her conversation with Annie on hold. Annie shivers in disbelief staring at her mother's youthful naked back. The angular figure caressing her mom's back looks directly at her through Vio's time loop. His deadly pallor does not harmonize with his keen, self-satisfied look. Annie gets a glimpse of him. She has seen him before. She cannot pinpoint when and where. He moves immediately after as if his goal has been satisfied. Vio returns to Annie, dissatisfied with their conversation.

"Do you think it was easy for me to know that my sole offspring spent hours on end wailing only to pass out exhausted from untamed fears?" Vio eventually continues her conversation with Annie and excuses her past acts by way of an explanation. "It was hellish, especially that you had nothing to fear. You were my daughter after all."

"Why didn't you tell me who I was? Had I had the knowledge of my enviable position I would have avoided going bonkers all those years."

"Annie, there were so many signs." "I saw none, grandma."

"If you insist. Start with me. No knuckles of old age. Nicholas had them."

"You looked very youthful, indeed." "My teeth were not porcelain."

"Indeed, old people had a glass with a scary denture on his bedtable. But that could have been good genes. Mom did not seem a day older than 20."

"You are a handful, kiddo. Okay. You loved eating tadpoles, for Christ's sake,"

Miriam interjects. "Anybody would have taken it as a hint you were … special."

"Mom, shush, Annie is right to be upset." And then after a moment of due silence, Vio adds, "I tried to make it up to you."

Annie remembers her mom carrying her small, limp body to the dinner table and waking her up with a kiss and smile in time for dinner, something quick and delicious.

"Couldn't you take time off? A maternity leave?"

"Annie, I was lucky to be considered good enough for Paris. And then, I love Paris."

"Without your mom the Ballets Russes would have left dhampir victims all over Paris, London, and New York. Vio is the best the West has got," Miriam adds with a tremolo in her voice.

"Mom, that's so generous and … unlike you." And then, jokingly, "Are you okay? Oh, I forgot, you're …sort of dead."

No one laughs at Vio's joke. Annie's becoming suddenly sullen.

"Mom, it's getting harder and harder for me to make sense of my life. For all my youth I had no idea about humans, dhampirs, dhampires and vampires. I did not know that vampires bite humans and sometimes those infested humans reproduce a half-human half-vampire offspring, a dhampir, who usually is still- born but who apparently has found Russia and some surrounding areas propitious to their survival on animal blood."

"Annie, dhampirs are degenerate beings. They cannot control their unnatural attractions to humans. Bitten humans become both ill and contagious to other humans. Their most noticeable symptoms are the epileptic seizure and the telepathic connection with their prey."

"Dhampirs, like their human parents are very attractive, kiddo."

"I know grandma. We, dhampires, are the product of such attraction between vampires and dhampirs."

"Yes. We remain immortal, like our vampire parents, but our powers change. Water and sunlight do not affect us, but we can only fly through time and space if they have an assignment, a memory call, or a relative opens a time and space loop inviting them to connect."

Annie s uncomfortable.

"Mom, now that I am immortal, do I have to be forlorn too?" She picks at her fingernails. Miriam's fate takes over her thoughts.

"Annie," Miriam calls on her, in an attempt to interrupt the fast reel impressing on Annie's senses. Dhampires relive memories as live theater unfolding in front of their eyes, while repressed memories or rumors pass by their eyes as a fast forward film.

Annie's body jerks backwards as she hears and explosion and a fire lights the night sky. Her grandparents' two-story house tumble down. In the midst of the rubble, she can make up two silhouettes lying down. The image she sees zooms in. Time lapses. The fire is gone. The dark is all encompassing. Sirens are approaching. Annie sees herself barely ten years old stumbling on a pitchfork. Annie's moves seem controlled.

"Silly Putty, you did it!" reverberates and the movie ends.

"Annie," Vio brings Annie back into the present, "What did Dan want?"

"I'm not sure," Annie stands up visibly shaken by her vision. She forces herself to make small talk, "He is back in my life."

"He called you a few times. Probably out of boredom."

"Until I decipher Dan I am stuck with him." No one contradicts her, so when she almost screams "get used to me trying to understand him," her reaction is unexpected.

"Kiddo, only humans engage in histrionics." Miriam makes herself heard.

"Grandma, please leave me alone. I cannot see you dead and hear your voice as if you were alive."

"Annie, dearest, can't you move on with your beautiful life, child?" Vio makes her plea.

"Until I get Dan I feel lost, unanchored."

"Kiddo, don't let yourself bamboozled. By anybody. Are you sure Dan called you?"

Miriam's words take a while to sink in. They feel both right and strange. Who else could have called?

Vio does not react. Her attention is refocused on the party. Her guests are dancing. Jazz has crossed the ocean and is bringing Parisians to their knees. Lev seeks Vio's company. She hands him a cigar instead, and asks him to make sure there is still plenty of caviar. Time for more champagne. Later the desert.

"It is not working out that easily, is it, Annie?" Vio's voice is trying a different approach.

"No, mom, it's not," Annie replies as she peeks outside the blinds. She notices shapes in the light outside her window. Faces become noticeable, too. She has never really had any interest in people whether as food or otherwise. Only in individuals. Blood has never occupied much of her time. She's been vegan since her kiss. She could have dodged reconnecting with Dan multiple times, but doggedly, she has refused to do so.

When she recognized his "Alo," the Romanian for "Hello," back in April, she refused to show weakness and hang up.

"Annie," he continued skipping the greetings, "Tell me, my dear Annie, are you happy?" It took her a moment to recover from the directness of his question delivered with great evenness:

"If you're asking me whether I have two legs and two arms and they all function well, then the answer is yes," Annie replied, though she meant "the nerve you have."

And then, they finally set a date to meet. A long-foretold date, she thinks. So long, that Annie doubts it happened.

"This is great news," Miriam whispers through Vio's time loop. "She is not sure they met."

Annie recalls Dan's call asking her out for a stroll in Central Park. She closes her eyes and sees herself a month ago, in April waiting for him in Central Park. She does not feel good about the walk. Too many people making themselves available in the empty meadows. "What if I lose my self- control?"

"Mom, where is she going with this memory?" Vio sends Miriam her worrisome thoughts as she is sitting down between Sasha and Lev. They all savor their inebriating drinks thinking at the night ahead; with whom each will celebrate the triumphant first show of the 1909 Parisian season. Vio finds a seat and watches the guests silently, pale, like a schoolgirl waiting for her mother's reply.

"I'm afraid there is nothing we can do except to watch and try to distract her."

Annie reads her text. "Outside the subway station. I'm not alone." She watches a couple. He, very tall and rather imposing.

She very tall and rather imposing too. She must be Alicia, his current wife, companion and confidant, takes all comfort away from Annie. Pondering what to do, to show off her teeth or to put on her gloves, because it is a cold April evening after all, Annie goes WASP.

"Are you okay, Annie?" Miriam asks her. She jumps at her words and touches him. Next to him she looks lost. Maybe she has shrunk. She does not remember him so tall. Having lost her voice, she keeps her fists tight. She is making a supreme effort to keep her teeth tight. She is fighting an indescribable desire to bite to feel warm blood. She closes her eyes for a moment. She cannot control herself.

"Annie feels the pressure of the past, twice remembered: the last spring encounter and the one three decades ago," Miriam whispers to Vio.

"Can we help her? Try something mom?"

Miriam blows cold air on Annie's neck. "Grandma?" Annie asks. A tickle in her ear, her grandmother whispers "fatso" taking all the tension away from the moment. His truly imposing body outside the subway stop takes over their butchered April date. Suddenly Annie remembers her first encounter with Dan, in 1988 far better than their last, in April, 30 years later. "A time burp," using her grandmother's verbal dowry.

"Do you see how the past only repeats itself? Last spring was like Podunk, 1988. You cannot change anything. You can only relive your pain, kiddo." Annie nods.

"You are right, grandma. I do not want to relive my pain."

Vio smiles. Lev takes her smile as meant for him and returns it politely. She excuses herself that she needs to make a private call. From her Parisian terrace overviewing the Seine, she can finally breathe relieved.

"Annie, please don't do it."

"She cannot help herself. Something is happening to her."

Annie closes her eyes shut until it pushes away the April memory for the earlier, 1988, Podunk remembrance. Their kiss. That memorable time. Dan's eyes, gloriously dark, marked by the longest eyelashes that side of the Danube, shining arrogantly, dominated her world entirely, and made everything else a mere ornament.

"We are safe," Miriam whispers. "For now," Vio agrees.

Not as popular as she would have liked to be in senior high and ignorant of her dhampire heritage, Annie goes to Collin's 18th birthday. "White trash," as Annie has discovered, is not the worst label for those living in the public houses by Gypsy Town. Her neighborhood, too. Luckily, there is no rule that poor people have to put up with undesired fondling by their peers' parents, so when

Annie pushes away Collin's inebriated father, she has to swiftly close the entrance door behind her and skip several stairs on her flight outside.

Insulted and sullen, worried about consequences she could not foresee, Annie stares ahead without really seeing anything. Except hearing. She can hear the giggles in Collin's apartment, and the way she's described as "foolish" and "stupid," for throwing away such blessed attention from the director of the local hospital. She's been replaced. There is no need to hurry, though she starts running.

She crosses the street away from Collin's apartment complex towards the side of the forest residents have made into a park, by placing a bench here and there, only in dark places, involuntarily enabling population control: the local dhampir population flourished on a diet of mortals.

She almost trips over him and stops.

"Hey, so you know how to run. You should join the track team." Dan mocks her in a brotherly way. "Why the speed? No one's following you. Don't you know that by now?"

Annie recognizes his voice. Dark, she can only imagine the smirk that goes with it.

Bravely, he approaches her. He leans on her. He is drunk. Or his mouthwash has had more alcohol than Johnny Walker.

"You look sadder than usual, as if that could be possible. What the hell is going on with you, Annie? You always look as if you're ready to cry when I'm around." He lights his lighter.

"Collin's father made a pass at me" Annie explains herself. "I knew I should not have come tonight." Annie keeps talking.

"Brave girl. Not even my squeeze pushed away Old Collin's advances."

Not even inches apart, Dan gently moves her face nearer. Their breathing becomes incestuous. His eyelashes touch her. Electricity shoots through Annie's body.

"It'll be okay," he whispers sensing her tremor.

The full moon, out from behind clouds, fills the space between them with uncharted hopes. Annie isn't sure her heart has ever pounded so fast in her life. In the moonlight, she notices a small scar on Dan's neck. For a fleeting moment she wonders how he got it. She has always wanted to know everything about him. And more than anything, she wants to feel his lips on hers.

"Silly Putty," Nicholas's voice is suddenly echoing.

Vio hears it from her Parisian terrace. Miriam hears it from her grave.

"Nicholas talked to Annie that night. They communicated. How is that possible, mom?"

"My child, that's a mystery for you to find out."

Vio turns towards Annie's 1988 daydream. Dan's lips meet Annie's, and she stops playing being alive. She feels alive. She feels her age: 17 years old. The warmth of his mouth sends a current running through her body. Without thinking, Annie throws her arms around Dan's neck and she loses herself in his soft lips totally and irrevocably inebriated by his Johnny Walker breath.

"The kiss. Her first kiss. Mom, I cannot watch it."

Annie touches her lips instinctively. They are wet. The liquid is not saliva. She does not know whose blood that is. They search for a sign from the other. His eyes look blank. Her eyes and face are on fire. She tastes blood. Her suddenly elongated teeth might have shocked him sober, waking him up from his adolescent stupor.

"Uh…I have to go," he says, stepping back to create space between him and Annie. "I don't want to be late. My parents always wait to have dinner with me." But he does not budge from his spot. He looks at Annie, but Annie is not her old self anymore. She has started her new evolutionary step. She is moving inwardly.

"Here comes the moment when Annie finally understands how enviable her position in the world is." Miriam narrates and her time loop evaporates.

The taste of blood turned on an internal switch in Annie. Her eyes become shut, encompassing everything. She discovers her powers: she could see what was happening far away in space and back in time. She sees her mother staring at her from a luxurious terrace located probably in Paris, but not the Paris of the smuggled 1980s magazines circulating on the Romanian black market of her adolescence. Vio looks the part of the hostess in a black and white Garbo movie from the 1930s when Annie's time loop opens in her apartment making Annie's first kiss visible to her. Vio shoves Vatsa out of the way and rushes out to rescue her daughter.

"Mama, I'm fine," a bloody young Annie pushes her mom away.

Dan, the son of the local morgue director has enjoyed kissing Annie.

"Annie," Dan shivers as he could imagine his mother spitting her name with disdain. The kiss has not empowered him with any knowledge. He's the same adolescent in love with himself who enjoys girls' attention. That kiss was awesome. Annie bit him and he bit her back. Annie, the brainiac from the worst public house in Podunk, the one behind the railroad station, "in the middle of Gypsy country," as Dan's mom loves to joke, will make a great bed companion one day, he thinks, and Annie can hear him. Her blood is boiling. "Annie could never dream of becoming your girl, Dan, don't you give her any hopes." Annie further hears Dan's mother lecturing him. "Can you fancy the social outrage? Her mom calls herself Vio. Why? Is she a flower, a violet? And what does she do after work? Vio visits orphanages and complains if any Gypsy orphan goes missing without proper adoption papers. Is she a Gypsy orphan herself? And what does that make Annie? A half Gypsy? No way, Dan, you will never touch that trash of a girl."

Annie can hear Dan mother's eternal scolding. "Silly Putty, don't do it."

"Mom, that was Nicholas's voice again," Vio tries to connect with her mom, but Miriam's time loop is shut down. Annie's memory call is going on, and Vio cannot ignore it,

"I don't know what happened here tonight." Dan's worrisome face melts away. "Do you think we can forget about it?" He asks sincerely sober.

"Of course," Annie manages to respond, only too late. Turning on his heels, he practically sprints out of the park. Left alone Annie cannot believe Dan has kissed her! "Wait! " She calls. "Life is great." She echoes her feelings with one small word. "Dan!"

"Sweetheart, it's over."

Annie shakes her head in disbelief. Weighed down by memories, she sits up slowly into her office leather chair. The smell of fresh leather has stopped irking her.

"Come back to me," Vio sends another invitation. "Leave behind New York City. Come be with me, my child. You don't have to share my Parisian quarters. I have a chateau in Provence." Annie acquiesces for a break.

"Mom, I have a funny feeling that something does not add up."

"Let it go, Annie. Come to me. Let me take care of you. Let me redeem myself."

Annie seems to consider the invitation. She stands up and starts walking. She takes the express back in time. Vio is relieved. It says, "Back to Podunk." Miriam sighs loudly "oy." Diaghileff turns toward Vio and calls out to her:

"Princess de Polignac, cette soirée est inoubliable," and smiles with a slight bow.

Vio smiles back and disappears in the tobacco smoke. She needs to watch over Annie's memories. The musicians hired for the night start playing some quieter Debussy to the delight of Sasha who soon seeks Claude in the select crowd.

***

3 THE CHICKEN OR THE EGG?

It's a short walk in time from New York 2016 to Podunk, early 1970s. More like one giant step and Annie is surrounded by the noise of children running and screaming with the joy of dinner being cooked for them only yards away. Startled by a honking horn, Annie turns around to see a small car, a beige Trabant, coming to a halt. Trabant, the little East German car built under the stasi regime was a status symbol: the Romanian state trusted the driver's skills sufficiently with a Duroplast vehicle, combining a form of hardened plastic made of cotton waste from Soviet Russia and resins.

"Mom, what is Annie up to now?"

"Nothing to worry about. She's back in time. Back into her childhood. She is exploring her life."

"I think we stopped communicating some decades ago."

"The eternal generational barrier. The good news is that it goes away once you reach one hundred." Miriam laughs. A hollow laugh a little nimble girl of no more than three, with a head full of strawberry blond curls, does not hear.

"Daddy, Tifaru!" She screams and trips on her patent leather shoes a size or two bigger. She does not cry and up, slightly bleeding from her knees she rushes again. Her

orange dress with pink flowers somehow enhances her strange beauty. "Gramps, Gigi!" is lost in the engine noise.

As she comes within reach, one of its two male passengers, both dressed in beige suits, matching the car's shade, opens his door and arms. The little girl is trapped.

"Daddy, Tifaru."

"Annie, who came first the chicken or the egg?" Tifaru asks grabbing little Annie.

His scent is so pleasant; Annie forgets the question:

"I'm so happy you don't smell like Gabe's dad."

"How does Gabe's dad smell," Gigi, sitting behind the wheel sounds curious.

"Like sweat," she says attempting to escape Tifaru's embrace. Tifaru emanates a citrusy scent. It fits so well with his suit's shade of beige.

"Who came first, the chicken of the egg?" Tifaru lifts her and throws her into the air.

"Uncle Gigi," Annie squeaks with pleasure.

Gigi turns off the ignition key, and comes out looking intent to joining in the horseplay. There is no place for him between Annie and Tifaru, so he retreats back into his car.

"I'm too old for this type of fun. It will break my back," he announces his change of mind.

"You're not old, Gigi," Tifaru interrupts and placing Annie on the ground goes to Gigi. His gaze is so tender that Annie does not know whether she's expected to go away and give them some privacy or just be quiet and wait for the moment to go. Ignored, Annie goes around,

"Daddy Tifaru, why are you lying?" Annie asks despondently, "Look, your hair is all dark and curly, while grandpa, sorry, uncle Gigi's hair is white and almost all gone."

Gigi, white-haired, and bi-spectacles, a small frame with a funny name, suddenly stares at the little girl slightly bemused. Uncomfortable, the child runs away. Gigi turns on the ignition key and takes off, almost running her over. Annie, all grown up, retreats into her time loop back in New York.

"Why are you bothering with those two?" Miriam's voice welcomes her back in the cold office.

Annie shrugs off the question. Her mind goes in swirl. A gossip unfolds and she sees a much younger Gigi and an old adolescent Tifaru facing each other. They do not blink. They smile. Gigi is shorter. He bends. Tifaru's in ecstasy. A few moments later a security guard arrives with a man in a blue pantsuit. The reel seems scratched. Something is wrong. The surroundings look like a public bathroom. Then, Annie sees Gigi and Tifaru dressed immaculately, and sitting in front of a panel of blue-suited men. Gigi explains that the other stools do not have toilet paper. A few moments later a big meeting takes place in the university main auditorium. A standing man reads something from a piece of paper. Tifaru cries. The Communist Party expels both of them and punishes them to community service in Podunk at a recently built factory lacking the proper informing structure. Moments later Annie sees them in their HR office. They exchange not a filial kiss behind the close door of their office.

"Miriam, how can I see a drop of blood on Tifaru's collar, if this was a rumor?" It does not make sense. "Who would have been able to tell me that Gigi had bitten Tifaru before mom met him?"

"Kiddo, why don't you put it all aside," Miriam's voice tries to be soothing while opening a time loop from New York to Paris. Vio needs to see what Annie sees.

Sunday memories from her early youth flood Annie visually. Back in the early 1970s, she spots Gigi's car on the highway from her bedroom window. She runs out and reaches the parking lot next to their courtyard as the car was coming to a halt. She goes to Gigi who rolls down his window and handed her a little two-inch doll – a nicely wrapped up gift. She squeals filled with happiness. Tifaru comes out from behind having made no noise. He picks her up and throws her into the air asking her the cosmological question about the primacy of the chicken or of the egg. His question is the same every week, but Annie will playfully change her riposte:

"The rooster," she replies then. Still holding her, Tifaru

goes around the car, picks up his beige leather briefcase and then around to Gigi and wishes him good night with a filial kiss through the driver's window. Holding both Annie and his briefcase under his arms, Tifaru turns towards the public housing whistling. He fishes out of his pocket a plain bagel perfectly wrapped in tin foil and handed it to Annie gently as if he were a medieval knight handling some holy grail.

"It's still warm," Annie screams full of pleasure and gratitude, escaping Tifaru's hold. She hurries up the stairs ahead of him, through the pitch-dark stairwell. She does not ring the bell; the door is open. Inside, she goes directly to the kitchen. Vio is the image of the perfect mother, sporting an apron, and cooking dinner on high heels and fully manicured, "Mom, do you want a bite?"

"I would like my own bagel," Vio invariably mutters and hands Annie a wooden spoon with an encouragement to lick it and see if the food is ready to be served.

Annie refuses opening her little mouth to take a huge bite of the bagel.

"Please don't eat it now; it would spoil your hunger."

Pouting, Annie leaves the bagel on the table and moves into the living room. Another Sunday memory. A year later.

Tifaru's feet smell terribly. Perhaps the nylon beige socks are to be blamed. Annie opens the door to the terrace and sits down at the living room table. The TV sports show cover a bit of Niki Lauda, a bit of Cassius Clay, their biggest hero. Tifaru jumps out of the sofa up and directs her gaze:

"Look at his feet, Annie, look how nimble and elegant he is. Look how precisely his fist moves toward his opponent's face."

"Why do you go to Bucharest every Saturday?" Annie asks Tifaru. For a moment Tifaru remains unsure about what he should say next.

"Do you know what he said after he won gold in Rome in 1960?"

"Why do you go to Bucharest every Saturday?"

"No, he said: 'To make America the greatest is my goal, So, I beat the Russians, and I beat the Pole, and for the USA won the medal of gold.' And then the Italians said: 'You're Greater than the Cassius of old. We like your name, we like your game, So, make Rome your home if you will.' And he continued: 'I appreciate your kind hospitality, but the USA is my country still, 'cause they're waiting to welcome me in Louisville.'"

"Why are you going to Bucharest every Saturday?"

"Do you miss me when I'm gone?" Tifaru replies avoiding the question.

"Dinner's served," Vio puts her head in the doorway beckoning them to join her around the kitchen table.

Tifaru turns off the TV and follows Annie to the bathroom where they both wash their hands. "Mommy and I had dinner while lying on your couch while we watched the Saturday night movie and I fell asleep." Tifaru nods his head encouraging her to continue. "Mommy let me sleep, and you know what? I didn't get scared the entire night. I slept through," Annie explains with the sincere enthusiasm of a child ignorant at the effect of her words.

"Got it now? I leave to make you happy," Tifaru enlightens his audience and they finish their dinner quietly.

When Cassius Clay wins the 1974 championship, he has become Muhammad Ali, an anti-war hero. Tifaru lectures Annie,

"Annie, this is historic. Symbolically this is a larger blow to the United States' imperialism and its cowboy hats and pointed boots than any Brezhnev Nixon arms ban treaty meeting." Annie looks lost. Emboldened Tifaru tells her in one breath how the United States was drafting all those young beautiful boys making them into cannon meat. He stops. "The world should belong to those who have the courage to stand up for their beliefs," Tifaru adds, "not to people … like me."

He rushes to the kitchen. Annie follows him. Standing in front of an open refrigerator drinking directly from the one-liter bottle of plum brandy, he silently cries. It takes him a while, until he collapses on the kitchen floor. Intimidated, Annie does not move until Vio comes home smelling of

Eau d'Hadrien and carrying a box of candied chestnuts.

"Annie, why are you focused on Tifaru?"

"Just reminiscing." "That unhappy."

"Unfulfilled mostly."

"How would this stream-of- recollections help?"

Annie's too busy to reply. Decade-old gossip, overheard rumors, is currently unfolding like a celluloid film reel. Gigi and Tifaru are hosts. It is not her apartment. The house is spacious. It has a spiral staircase and doors which open and close and giggles come through. Tifaru is carrying an emaciated Gigi upstairs. A door opens and men, naked men, play poker and smoke fancy American cigarettes, and drink American whiskey. A woman, a naked woman, whom Annie recognizes and whose names she whispers, "Lauren," runs outside a door followed by Collin's dad. He is naked. Annie gasps for air and opens her eyes. She spots Vio in her Parisian penthouse taking another sip of Taittinger.

"Mom, have you kissed anybody?" Annie sends down her time loop a question for Vio's consideration, but she seems distracted with her guests. A new dancer whom she has not seen before or a new Dhampir. She encourages him. He comes to her and kisses her hand.

"Princess, I don't think we have been introduced," he says while Vatsa disregards any conventions, and talks louder than ever as he approaches Vio,

"Princess, I always wondered where this portrait would end up." Vio smiles and notices Diaghileff nodding at the willowy guest, now distancing himself from Vio. He is a prize from Lev.

"So happy you're pleased with the final effect," she replies to Vatsa and follows the newcomer. She reaches him as he is trying to leave her apartment. She takes his arm under hers and swiftly pushes him in a bedroom with a girlish giggle for whomever happens to notice her transient partner. Diaghileff is displeased but manages to smile as the door closes behind Vio. The orchestra has been instructed to start a jazzy piece whenever the host happened to retreat into a bedroom. The muffled scream is mostly unheard or if noticed, it is translated in pure eroticism by the less knowledgeable partygoers.

"Did you kiss grandpa Nicholas?" Annie sends her question down the other time loop, one ending in Radeş. After centuries of never-ending parties, Miriam led a life of peasant domesticity, until her demise.

"Of course." "And?"

"Our family ran away for our dear life every century or so," Miriam starts the answer.

"I'm sorry."

"Don't. We got to know Europe pretty well," Miriam says and chuckles. "When we arrived in Radeş, I was looking Nicholas' age. He was about 18, and so lean and muscular that I knew I wanted him. We were running for our lives, when we had to stop at the inn for the night. The inn belonged to his family."

"People still referred to your Radeş home as Miriam's tavern."

"Nicholas insisted to call it that way. Strangely, thinking back, it was all a blur. I vaguely remember my parents retiring to their room. I was left to get acquainted with my new family. Dad telepathically ordered me. Nicholas cooked and served the food not once taking his eyes off me." Miriam's voice sounds chocking with tears. "He cut his fingers once but ignored the cut and continued cooking."

"You ate his blood?"

"Probably. It was cooked though."

"I still don't understand why you stayed."

"I was tired of running away."

"It does not make any sense."

"Sorry kiddo. Life does not always make sense."

"I have a nagging feeling that it is all a puzzle, if I can only put the pieces together."

"Two pieces of the puzzle are buried in Radeş."

"Did you kiss Nicholas? "

"Annie, I made love to him that night and many more afterwards. I did not stay for the food. Come and visit me before 1977."

"You know we cannot talk about what has not happened. You died when I was barely 7. My first kiss won't happen until junior high. Why shall I come?"

"Kiddo, you are a Dhampire. Come and relive your talks. Amnesia is not in your cards." After a brief silence, Miriam adds, "Of course, we cannot talk about the future, but often the future is in the present."

Annie is distracted by another memory. She hears a black Mercedes stopping across the parking lot, at the gas station near her public housing apartment. She steps back in her time loop to Podunk 1973.

The adult behind the wheel sprints out to fill in the tank. He is lean and dark and sports a mustache long enough to cover an everlasting smirk. In the dead man' seat there is a youth, not long past his toddler years. He puts his dark, chubby face out the window and stares towards Annie. His eyelashes are so big they create waves of warm air when he blinks. He must be seeing her younger self in a game of who-blinks- first-loses. Soon he's smiling and retreating into the car closing the window. She has time to notice his candy-rotten teeth. Annie hears her younger self vowing to stop brushing hers too.

It's their first encounter.

"Kiddo, you proved me wrong. You got something out of your parking lot walk."

"I know grandma." Annie smiles wondering if Miriam could see her or just hear voices. "I used to have this memory of Dan standing alone in the kindergarten courtyard. Like a little owl, or a very young Heathcliff. He was wearing a blue uniform both too large and too wrinkled. I used to wonder whether fatigue, ennui or mere lack of entertainment, made me go to him pushing past Gabe and Mia, my neighbors from the public housing. I did not stop until I reached him. Now I know why I took his hand, soft and moist and pulled him toward the old walnut tree without a word. I was reaching out to a new friend." Annie stops her reminiscence. "I was taking care of a snail family. And I was working on an artificial pond, so tadpoles would like coming with me to school, one day."

"How did he react?" asks Miriam.

"I don't remember," Annie replies wondering how much truth her answer contains.

***

4 PUBLIC HOUSING TADPOLES

Vio leans over looking at the sidewalk below. Only six stories above the ground.

"You're acrophobic?"

"Yes," she replies without turning. He caresses her hair freeing her face. Or trying to. The Parisian morning breeze is chilly, but so refreshing. The musicians are gathering their instruments. The last song lingers in her mind. She did not pay attention to it because it sounded uncouth and aside from being an overnight sensation she would have never allowed Max Dearly and his dancing partner Alexis, to engage in their violent, Apaches, dance, or rather pantomime. They peppered the percussion butchered waltz with slapping and pushing and dragging each other, as if they were working through a stylized domestic fight between two savage lovers. Sasha found it demented. Vatsa loved it. He took notes.

"Did you enjoy the after-party party?"

"How many times have you been able to come up with something new to celebrate the Ballets Russes 1909 debut?" Vio ignores his question. She murmurs the latest melody heard. Stuck to her mind because of its dark, circus-like undertone. "The Parisian hooligans' dance was terrific."

"I discovered Max and Alexis at the Moulin Rouge in La Revue du Moulin. For half a century I have been stuck in

1909 and I just saw La Revue du Moulin." Vio explains.

The servants are cleaning the terrace. Princesse Edmond de Polignac detests flowers or any kind, roses or gardenias. Strangely, they will bring new ones in a few hours, when the revelry will start anew as if it never happened.

The sun in rising above the roofs. Vio yawns.

"Your Bedouin tent is ready if you want to follow me," Vio's companions holds her shoulders in a comic paternal way. Though both are thin and willowy, he also looks unwell to be taken seriously. Vio rests her head on his shoulder. He gingerly takes her away from the edge of the terrace and brings her away from the sun. He has time to check on Annie, still visiting her childhood in Podunk, before Vio's time loop shuts down.

Stuck in the parking lot behind the betony hippopotamus, which her apartment building resembles, Annie seems to gather her wits and starts walking around. She takes the gravel paved path along grassy patches, but mostly dirt. She turns. The train station in visible now. She ignores it captivated by the apartment building where she spent almost 18 years incredibly sad and fearful and tender and hopeful, and above everything else, where she abandoned her youth while never thinking it was hers forever. The small windows and even smaller terraces, as if their purpose was to bear the inquisitive eye of the dutiful neighbor, any curious neighbor, beckon at her and Annie finds herself released in her youth at her own recognizance. She won't mess around the courtyard or the architectural behemoth. No one would. The collections of apartments placed on top of each other in the most functional way in the minimal amount of time demand respect as only large bodied strangers impose. There is no possibility of communication so distance becomes a friendly gesture.

Through the green poplar leaves, the white painted construction, whose plaster is mostly chipped off, as it should be at its advanced age, still appears inviting. Like the witch's ginger house. With Gretel's lack of care, Annie reaches the entrance. The heavy metal door wide open brings to mind fire escapes.

Inside, the smell of fried onion pervades her senses. And chicken liver, and "mămăligă," the cornmeal mush associated with all her meals, which soon replaced everything else for her whenever eating outside the confines of her apartment. To, "Annie, what would you like?" she invariably replied, "Just mămăligă, please," to the approval of whatever adult supervision the dinner would have. She still uses that excuse.

The staircase is as dark. She remembers the light bulb securely nested in its socket never worked. The adult residents grew content to look up at the ceiling and see it there. No one ever dreamed of picking up a ladder or a chair, climbing up on it and looking at the darn thing up close to see why it did not do its job of piercing the eternal thick darkness with a show of light and shadows. Doing so would have been silly. The landlord, the Romanian soviet state, did not have spare light bulbs for the commons, or maybe it just wanted all four floors to share the same frigid darkness. A rascal of a boy runs by, oblivious to her presence, further reminding Annie of her childhood, when neighboring kids joyfully returning from a day of schooling, ran up and down the stairs eventually reaching their apartment and blindly fitting their key in their door locks, ending the metallic dangling noise with a human scream: "Mom!" as soon as they were in. It was not the beginning of a complaint of the over- encompassing darkness. It was instead of hello. An equally loud mom or grandma or aunt, as if lurching around or frying onions in the kitchen, would come for a brief moment to check the state of their offspring and then run back to frying the onions.

Annie gets pushed by another rascal sliding down the handrail. As she remembers, no one slid alone. The fun was in the numbers. And most every child loved the handrail. The fastest and most acrobatic way down the dark stairway. If ever admonished, the scoundrels could blame the darkness for using the stair handrail to glide down in seconds. "Sorry!" they would say as they passed old ladies, someone's still useful grandma breathing heavily while carrying basic groceries: a loaf of bread, a bottle of skimmed milk, and maybe 100 grams of butter, up the stairs. The little devils would scare the pour soul and force her to retreat by the wall as they - irrespective of gender. Accidentally, perhaps, but surely content they impersonated the Lost Boys tumbling down their underground holes.

Eventually, she reaches the second-floor landing. One more floor to go! The same old feeling pushing her each time she climbed up the stairs. On the right stood Lauren's apartment, "Gary's girl," as she was called though Gary was not her real father; he only had her father's age, probably. Next to hers was Mia's apartment, her eternal frenemy. How silly, Annie smiles and keeps going. Then, the twins, Sandy and Robert, and their mother lived in the largest apartment in the building. She wonders how they had money for the triple rent. She is ready to turn when she remembers Fini. On the left as, she walked up the stairs, lay Fini's apartment. Little, emaciated, meek raisin Fini whom she found often in her living room demanding the attention she never commanded outside that table.

If Lorazepam ruled the soviet nights, Turkish coffee was the queen of the day. A few times a week, sometime between four and five in the afternoon, perhaps after a brief nap at the end of a demanding morning of teaching, Ella, and Dina, her mom's colleagues and friends, came by for a cup of coffee and a moment of joy. Vio always baked or fried or assembled some desert to greet them. When she would do all that, Annie had no clue. Sometimes, Russian coffee cake, or fried beignets "exactly as Tennessee Williams liked them," Vio would introduce them and no one thought twice of how awkward that detail sounded. Most often, Vio served crepes filled with home- made jams.

"Vio, you really know how to make coffee the way the Turks served it when they owned the land," Ella the historian would often compliment Vio while sipping carefully. "It is the Turkish coffee pot, the copper ibrik, that makes the difference." That was often the cue to refresh the coffee.

Fini was sitting upright frowning at a hardened grained of coffee supposed to bring light on the future of the believer. Annie ignored the drama developing at her living room table. Annie closes her eyes to enjoy the view of Fini's slightly dirty worn- out outfit, and her thin receding hair, hardened by molding spray, all rolled up, and presented to the world as if a plate of stuffed cabbage. The white roots woven with brown ends had less of a rejuvenating effect than advertised. Fini demanded everybody attention, and following the ingestion of Turkish coffee, she usually got what she wanted.

Embarrassed for taking pleasure in such old memories, Annie hurries up the stairs. She slows down as she almost slips. Someone dripped oil on the stairs. She stops to think if she could remember where the commons' broom and bucket were located. Each floor had one closet. She turns to open the door and stops. She can see through the locked door that it has been transformed into a habitable room. She steers away from that spot: infested with Dhampir prey.

On the third floor's landing Gabe's apartment stood across from hers, with two others, which she had never visited tucked in between. Her apartment is on the right. Its door has the same shade of unhealthy green, probably lead-based, probably provided by the landlord. She opens the door, now metallic. Inside, the railroad apartment with one room following the other looks even less spacious than she remembers it. Maybe the walls, abrasive, cold, and impersonal, turn her off. The kitchen, on the left from the hallways, right near the entrance, smells of Clorox. Annie shivers. Vio never used Clorox. She moves further. The living room has no sofa. The current occupants seem to treat it as its name indicates, and spend their lying down time in the next room, the bedroom, located at the other end, next to the bathroom.

An intense feeling of doom closes down on her. She runs to the bathroom and vomits, or goes through the vomiting motions. Nothing comes up and out. She has not eaten in quite some time. She flushes and stands up wiping her face. Her movements are reflected back in the mirror. The toilet is ready to overflow. The smell of feces and Clorox compete with no winner in sight. She carefully takes a towel and throws it on the floor so she can step out carefully. Neither revulsion nor embarrassment. She could have kept her past zipped up and sealed away from reach. She hasn't. Watching herself in the mirror she hears some screaming and banging coming out of the bedroom. She runs only to answer another memory call. The playful Sunday angel welcoming "Daddy Tifaru" back home is two years older and anger is her name:

"I want my bottle of milk," Annie screams over and over and over again. "Give me my sippy cup. Now!"

Sharing a Queen-size bed often is not the best situation for a mother and daughter to find themselves in. Faced with her mother's motionless body, Annie starts screaming and kicking her out of the bed. When on the hard parquet, Vio moans something and succumbs to either her daughter's demand, too tired and much reluctant of making an even louder scene for her neighbors. Within a few minutes she reappears with a bottle with warm milk. Annie grabs it with desperation. She is soon soothed into going back to sleep. Asleep, the five-year old looks so serene and content. Her previously bottled-up anger liquefied or re-absorbed for the following night.

"Had enough memory manure stuck on your shoe, Annie?" Miriam's voice breaks the spell.

"I wish," she replies. "But once released, their smell cannot be contained."

Retracing her steps back to the living room Annie notices a crack in the wall. She touches it. She knows when that crack appeared. As soon as she remembers it, a time loop opens and swoons her to the evening of the 1977 earthquake. She sits at the living room table doodling Dan's profile on a small piece of paper she keeps hidden in the homework book. She feels very sad.

Despondent. Dan's birthday party took place the day

before and she missed it. He's turned 7. She's still waiting her turn.

Dan invited all his classmates to his 7th birthday party. She wanted to make a statement. She chose a model Ferrari race car, which would have cost Vio her monthly wage as a Podunk teacher. The idea came to her when she went shopping for school supplies with her mom. She saw the Ferrari, the only model car in the entire general store, itself one of its kind in Podunk.

Forty years later she still remembers the thought process then as if it were today. Dan stopped talking to her afterward. Coincidence or not, Annie had to ask. She did last April.

"It happened four decades earlier, so, I really don't remember anything," he told Annie.

"So, you don't remember," she pressed the issue.

"Does it matter?"

"Of course. It means everything to me."

"Okay," he laughs or sounds as if he were amused, "if it matters so much to you, then you should imagine whatever happy ending you want. It is your story. "

Annie recoils. Dan is a little bastard, but the label does not satisfy mature Annie any more than it would satisfy a pre-teen Annie dreaming about him. She wonders how she aced all her school test when all her time is devoted to Dan.

Back in May 1977, the TV is on blasting. Tifaru is all drunk snoring on the coach. Annie would have missed the meaning of this phenomenon, has she not noticed the candelabra above her head becoming a pendulum of sorts. She asks Tifaru whether they should bang in the radiator to alert the neighbors that whatever they are doing is not good for their chandelier. Annie loves big words.

Woken up, Tifaru screams at her to turn off the TV, which she automatically does. He then runs out of the apartment, Barefoot. Happy to see him gone, Annie jumps on the couch away from the heavy chandelier, which looks corky and funny, but embarrassingly so out of place. Annie secretly prays to God it would not fall down and break when she's underneath it.

"Tifaru left without you?" Vio comes in and grabs Annie down from the sofa. Annie shrugs her shoulders.

"What's the big deal?" "What's the big deal?"

They start going down the stairs.

"Yes mom," Annie sounds worried but brave. For a brief moment the earthquake stops, and Vio has second thoughts. It restarts more powerfully. Neighbors are still going down and push them ahead. Outside, they are all safe. Tifaru is sitting on a bench with his head in his hands.

The following day, Tifaru brings her a notepad from the HR supply cabinet.

"Write, Annie."

"What, Daddy Tifaru? What shall I write about?" She wonders with her eyes fixated on the TV screen. She watches the Romanian President and his wife. She is braving the rubble in high heels to find earthquake survivors. She tells the reporter she can only wear Gucci shoes, and so far she has destroyed four pairs. Annie thinks fast. She must change her shoes a few times each day. She looks at her feed. Bare.

But Annie starts writing about the President and his wife digging for survivors under the rubble, and getting bitten by bats and becoming vampires and talking to the dead and finding the survivors or not.

"What happened to your novel? Did it have a plot, or just laudatory words about the presidential couple?" Vio surprises Annie by using her time loop.

"The novel did not get finished."

"What do you mean it did not get finished?"

They both visualize the fate of the novel. Ella opens it once and with fidgety fingers flips the pages, not that many, reads the brief sentences and looks at the drawings. Annie loves comic books. She then laughs, "Vio, you are not bringing up a communist," she adds closing the notebook. She then places her coffee cup upside down too, to dry out the grains, so Fini could read her future. When Annie discovers the deed from the circles of coffee the cup left on it, she brings it to a recycle center to set an example. Even a few grams could differentiate the honor pioneers from the rest.

"I must have gotten bored with the topic."

"No," Miriam interjects and her voice is received with a sigh. "Don't you remember? You told me when you came to visit for the summer. You found it marked with circles of dried out coffee grains, and you got mad. Ella used it by mistake to dry her coffee cup so Fini could read her future in its grain. You threw it in the garbage all insulted."

Both Vio and Annie smile at the lie. Annie does remember the exchange. That 1977 year had been intense then and even now reliving it. She retreats back in Podunk. The few years she has summed up were good. Good enough. She exists her apartment gingerly closing the door behind for fear not to wake up some lying memory dogs.

She does. Gabe's memory springs out at her. On the same floor landing, they went back a longs way: from the birth through high school. They must have seen each other in diapers, and Gabe must have seen Annie naked pieces of body through the off-white worn-out clothes when they played Sorry! at her place or his. Annie remembers seeing him in more compromising situations. She knocks at their apartment door. Her mom is out of sugar and she feels like baking. Annie resents being sent to neighbors to borrow stuff.

"Everybody did it," Miriam reminds her. True, but she disliked the bartering system of the soviet era.

While waiting for Gabe's mom to come and open the door, Annie hears some huge commotion inside. Gabe's parents are whispering on the other side of the entrance door. Annie hears "No, don't be foolish, Gabe doesn't have a tail."

Gabe's mom finally opens the door and there is Gabe, as curious as ever, out of the bathroom, nose running, and holding a rather big tape worm in his hand.

"Of course, this is not a tale; it is a worm," Annie hears him speak and his mother is all red and embarrassed and his father smells of sweat and attempts to close the door on Annie's face, when Annie starts laughing.

"I eat tadpoles," Annie says and Gabe starts laughing too, and somehow, his parents smile and his mom asks her to come in, and she does.

"Perhaps that was the first time we really talked," Annie mumbles and leans back on the stairwell wall. She can see the little man-made pond past the courtyard, past the parking lot, and across the highway. She superimposes her cherished memories of that time in early elementary school on the picture she has in mind of the pond. Not deep, maybe one foot, it was multifunctional. When it rains she gazes at the rain drops bouncing back from its surface until she gets all soaked. When it does not rain, she hunts for tadpoles and brings them home in a jar. When the water in the gigantic pool freezes, Annie slides up and down for hours, until her knees and hands hurt by so much scraping from cheerfully falling around.

Annie chuckles as she sees herself and Gabe collecting tadpoles in large glass jars, bring them home and watching them change from a mere big egg to a frog.

"They grow tales," Gabe gladly discovers one day. Annie mostly loves tenderly squishing their slimy little bodies. She giggles when they slip through her fingers and water splashes her when they're back in the jar. Gabe comes up with the idea of having lids with big holes. He uses a nail. He then stares at them through the holes. Annie reacts silently, "weird," as she stretches her arm, pushes her head of curly hair back and opens her fist straight above her open mouth. A fat tadpole vaults into her throat.

Gabe looks at her with a blank mind.

"You did not chew it." He observes. Annie agrees. "It may still come out of you alive." He continues. "Weird," Annie swallows and shrugs her shoulders.

Gabe's mom makes space for the jars in her well-lit pantry. Annie has an excuse to visit daily. In tadpole season, Vio's absences become tolerable. Every evening the two friends bring the jars to the pond. Gabe opens the lit and pours its content out into the pond. Then he fills it in with the catch. Annie's is empty. She bends and takes her time. She does not move as if gone.

"Hey Annie, I need to go home."

She nods and expertly moves the jars to catch what pleases her eye. They return to their apartment building happy to have borrowed a little splendor for a few hours. Walking up the stairs their faces are illuminated by the unlimited possibilities fastened tight in those jars. Transfixed. Beaming with pleasure, Gabe watches the little Frankenstein creatures swimming. Annie fishes out one and smiles.

***

5 SILLY PUTTY FACE BECOMES HER NICKNAME

"You never thought about ruining his life for having tried to ruin yours?" Annie blows her question into the wind of remembrance.

"Are you talking to me?"

"Who else? Mom is napping in her authentic Bedouin tent. I must ask her how she got it."

"Maybe you want to learn the answer to that question before you rephrase the one for me?"

"He cheated on you, didn't he?"

"Kiddo, that's unfortunate he confided in you. But there is so much more than that to a relationship, kiddo, and Nicholas helped me discover it all: the good and the bad, the ugly and the ugliest."

"Miriam, really, I am not interviewing you for any book of mine. He spent two years from June 1942 to August 1944 with someone else, and if I remember correctly he called her 'Odessa, the love of my life.' Didn't that kill you, grandma?" Miriam's voice is silent. Annie sighs. "I'm sorry. That was uncalled for. I guess I am in pain, confused, and lost. I try to cause pain to dead Dhampires to alleviate mine. I am pathetic."

"Nicholas had refused to be drafted. He was almost 60

years old. But I kept him young. Neither one of us looked a day older than 30. Your mom, Mary, as she was known in Radeş, was finishing her vigilante training and we had no one to point to confirm our age. No one believed us. Right before the big battle of Stalingrad. Everybody knew that the Germans were going to lose. They had no soldiers except forced drafts from the occupied countries and so-called allies. But they needed the conquest of Stalingrad. It was essential to their campaign in southern Russia. Stalingrad would have given them a strategic point on the Volga River to launch further assaults in the Caucasus."

"Grandpa Nicholas never made it." "No."

"When did you learn?"

"We were able to communicate telepathically. I could also hear his thoughts."

"I'm sorry grandma."

In Paris, a new day, a new challenge comes through Vio's newly opened time loop. Her assignment must have been the morning rehearsal for the Parisian 1909 debut. She wakes up one day back in time, and finds herself attending the final rehearsal for Tcherepnine's Pavillon d'Armide.

Maestro Cheketti lines up the dancers. Alexandre Benois, the librettist, is chatting with the pianist, Pomeranzev, who also plays the part divinely. Annie briefly forgets the nauseating chatter and tries to isolate the music from the noise. Karsavina, Baldina, and Nijinsky rehearse the pas de trois under careful attention of Michel Fokine. Nijinsky performs his elevation. Cheketti loves it. Karsavina is all gracefulness. Fokine's sharp eye takes it all in. Very much likes Vio's, who is sitting next to Jean Cocteau who elbows Anna de Noailles, Proust's "Princess from the East." Proust and Princess Yourbeletieff, sitting next to him with an immense feather hat, are non-stop talkers. Prince Myshkin comes in followed by a willowy man, whom he introduces as Cartel, a music critic for the Figaro. Now, Vio knows Robert Brussel, the Figaro music critic, a charming little man exuberantly though helplessly in love with Karsavina. Sasha stands up to serve himself with coffee, placed on a tray by the window, where Cartel and Lev are drinking theirs too. They chat. The chatter is unbearable. Fokine screams. "Out! Everybody out." Sasha smiles. Vio understands her challenge for the day. "Personne ne peut distraire les artistes," and Sasha looks around to see who can distract the artists at work. He looks around, makes eye contact with Vio, acknowledges her, and keeps going. His gaze stays with the new comer. "Sauf vous, M. Cartel," he finally says biting a deliciously buttered croissant.

"Annie, I have a story for you. Maybe that will help you understand. Do you remember the long walnut table under the old walnut tree?"

Annie nods and she immediately remembers sitting under that walnut tree with her grandfather not long after what she thought was his stroke, in early May 1977. The spring break that year came right after the earthquake. She spent two weeks in Radeş, that spring. At night, she would read aloud the newspaper or some history book lying on the ground next to her grandparents' bed. When done with the chores, she read the Battle of Stalingrad aloud, assuming that her war hero grandpa enjoyed reliving his glory. Then, when tired or bored she would turn on the radio and listen to music. Later at night they would watch a movie on TV. The same thing every night until one morning she decided to do it. When her grandmother was busy with breakfast, having finished feeding the animals, Annie, seven years old, approached Nicholas with an offer.

"Grandpa, would you trust me to shave you?" It was daring of her. Nicholas had a straight razor with an ivory handle.

The old man opened his eyes as brightly as he could. Someone could have seen it as a scared face. But Annie remained oblivious to his overstretched big eyes. She stared at the old man until he winked at her or just closed his eyes one at a time. "Good" she enunciated her satisfaction and went outside his bedroom to get started.

Confident that she could replicate the ritual she had witnessed so many times, she stood still appraising her future moves. The obstacle she could see was the hot water. There was no central heating in her grandparents' home. Resourceful, little Annie went downstairs, to the kitchen. Miriam was humming a catchy tune. Annie remained still until she recognized it. Cole Porter's S' marvelous. The answer found, she shared her decision with her grandmother who immediately liked it. While Miriam got the water ready, Annie located a bowl, the brush, soap, and the razor – a museum piece a bit rusted but very noble in its appearance. Annie visualized the ritual one more time: hanging the strop to smooth the rough edges off the blade and set them in perfect alignment, and then honing the blade, unused for so long, so its edges could be restored to their original condition. That would surely give the straight razor keen edges so shaving would become a breeze.

Satisfied with the preparations she returned upstairs to her grandparents' bedroom. She snuggled next to Nicholas for a while to give him courage. Then, she propped him up on three big down-filled pillows. Nicholas insisted on having his eye closed tight. It did not bother her. Meticulously, she soaped his beard while never stopping telling him stories about tadpoles, and Dan. How she missed the party of the year and she would probably never be invited again to any parties. She should get ready to die rather than go through with such a painful existence. Annie continued. Finally, she stopped talking when she could not recognize her grandpa underneath all that white foam. She kissed his forehead and got the razor. She stabilized herself and then opened it. She rested her first three fingers on the back of the blade, her small pinkie on the blade's tang, and placed her right thumb on the side of the blade near the middle. The shaving started in earnest. Her grandfather's eyes refused to watch her.

It did not take that long. When done, she caught herself humming S' marvelous. Her grandfather opened his eyes and smiled. She brought a mirror to him. Instead of a mangy dog, a good-looking septuagenarian was staring back.

"Thank you, Annie," he said without a stutter, as if the paralysis was gone. Annie loved to believe in magic and miracles thinking it were the effect of the shaving. She took his hand and helped him get off the bed. She brought him downstairs to the bathroom and then to visit with Miriam in the kitchen. Miriam was already gone to relax at the table under the walnut tree.

Yes, Annie nods, remembering the walnut tree fondly.

"When tired," Miriam continued, "I would sit down at the plain wood table under the walnut tree and blossom with life. I would use an old straight razor of Nicholas's and cut open a ripe peach, and take my time savoring each piece."

"Grandpa Nicholas's straight razor. I know what you mean," and she does.

"By the time I would sit down at that table he would have already been there for a moment or so. He would invite me to sit down with him. He would have a glass of cold lemonade and one of brandy. The straight razor out of his pocket, he would hand it to me. We would make eye contact and I would cut a peach in slices. Slowly. Never taking my eyes off him. He would remark how beautiful I was. I would just chew a piece of juicy peach and smile."

"I miss him."

"I know, kiddo. You two had a special relationship."

On such an afternoon her grandfather appeared to find a little wooden chess case filled with oily, barely recognizable pieces.

"Annie, I would like you to have it," he offered her the box.

Annie looked both happy and scared. She liked the present, but she did not know how to play chess. Such a competitive game in her apartment building, played in the stairwell within the light of the exit door so sunlight could keep the players in the know of their moves.

"Would you teach me?" She finally asked him.

"I am giving it to you so I will forget all about it." Nicholas added without making eye contact. Annie's flushed face might have emanated discomfort. He looked up and smiled. "Don't pout, Annie. Silly putty face, one day I will tell you more." And Silly Putty Face became her nickname.

And Nicholas continued to watch over Annie's growth that and a few more summers.

Chairs are shuffled and feet stamped. The Parisian fancy society does not like to be told to behave. Cocteau goes to Nijinsky. Fokine is in full anger. "Don't touch him," Fokine screams. Nijinsky is unclear about what that means. Vio goes to Fokine. She knows the power of persuasion her purse has. "M. Fokine, how would you and Mme Fokina like to vacation on my estate this summer?" Sasha turns towards her. Having tried in vain to remember how exactly she has managed to be among the upper crust of the chosen ones, now he understands. Lev whispers her name to him, "Princesse," Sasha starts. "M. Dhiaghileff," Vio replies. "How fortunate of us to call you a friend," he politely touches her gloved hand to his lips. "Tonight, you will delight me if you bring everybody to my place on Blvd St. Michele." Sasha is afraid to decline, but he has a soiree already organized. "Of course, after your pre-arranged party. Something simple. Champagne, and caviar, and a surprise." Vio adds and turns toward Fokine to hear his grateful acceptance for the summer vacation. "Of course, Princesse," Sasha adds, biting his moustache, unclear if he has accepted a magnanimous offer or has just fallen into a trap.

All quiet, Vio comes back to her seat. Both Cocteau and Proust are making space for her. She lends them each a hand and ceremoniously smiles at both. The rehearsal continues.

"Don't worry mom. I can manage." Annie decides to go back to her 1977 summer vacation.

She exits the train in Radeş, carrying a small bag with her huge notebook containing the adulatory novel dedicated to the Romanian president, at that time everybody's darling, a pencil box, and a few pieces of clothing. A pair of jeans attracts her stare. Probably because of the 12-hour train trip. Including the three connections. Each one lasting more than 2 hours. But, how and why? Never mind. The answer will come in due course.

"You're a good kid." Vio blows her an air kiss from the compartment's window.

"I'm seven, mom."

"Are you in a bad mood?" "Why can't I come with you?"

"Annie, here we go again. You know every kid needs to spend time with her grandparents. You are lucky my parents are still alive. Look at Tifaru's parents."

"Do you think I like being here for three months with Miriam's ticks?"

"Mom does not have ticks, does she?"

"Her chicken, dogs, cows, pigs, cats, rabbits, all her animals have ticks, mom."

"You love your grandpa."

"I don't know. He treats me so differently because of that shave."

"Annie, that was an amazing gesture of love you did for him. And you cured him of his … depression."

"Why can't I come with you?" Annie adds almost whispering. Vio hears her, but pretends she does not. She smiles and waves delicately as the train takes her safely away from Radeş.

Annie stands for a while on the platform looking at the departing train carrying her mother to a destination meant to relax her and give her some contentment: hot mud therapy. That thought cheers the little Annie enough and she starts the hike along the highway towards the village and away from the railroad.

She reaches her grandparents' house, back in 1977, visible from far away: the handsomest and tallest residence in that forgotten village on the southern side of the Carpathians. A few decades later it would be a different story: a pile of broken bricks.

"Your mom did not even stop to say thank you for babysitting her daughter during the entire summer." Miriam opens her mouth as soon as the door closes behind Annie, much to her surprise.

"Good to see you too, grandma," Annie replies and passes by Miriam quickly to enter the bedroom where her grandfather is still recovering from his stroke.

"Where is she? On her way to a summer of bile treatment?"

"Miriam, leave the child alone," Nicholas interferes with his frail voice. "You are scaring her," and turning to Annie. "Your grandma has changed so much. My doctor says she's burnt-out because of my illness. Please, don't mind her."

"I have worse bile problems than her. Whom does she think she is taking after? Me," Miriam addresses Annie.

"Silly putty, you made it again. Stand up close and let grandpa see how much you've grown since May!" Nicholas makes a conversation between Miriam and Annie impossible.

"You know you're not her grandpa."

Annie opens her eyes ending her recollection and standing up unbolts the window to her Columbia office. She craves the outside warmth: the air, the human giggle. Even the birds chirping.

"Miriam, why did you have to tell me that then? Do you know how much it hurt?"

Perhaps distracted with Nijinsky's vaults, Miriam's voice does not immediately reply.

"And why were you impersonating a crazy old hag to perfection?"

"I'm sorry, kiddo, Nicholas was deteriorating and trying to hurt you. Short of a coming out as a dhampire nothing seemed to work. Vio vetoed that in the most cowardly manner: she let me do the work."

"Mom did not want you to tell me who I was because what?"

"You were vey gullible at that age, Annie. Vampires usually do much more by 7 than eat tadpoles. Similarly, dhampires. You were very slow developing. I started believing in curses, and be afraid of Nicholas."

"Why?"

"He was obviously playing with me and you. He was not

the naïve human I thought him to be."

'By then you had spent almost seventy years together and you are telling me you did not know whether he was a human, a dhampir, or a dhampire?"

"I'm afraid so."

"And you are telling me that maybe he put a curse on me? Maybe Dan is my curse?" Annie cannot continue her train of thoughts. Meek and embarrassed, she seems to have only one option: to stand and pace up and down the office or to sit down and think about her life choices. She collapses inside and goes back to mid-June 1977.

"By the way, how is that pd of Tifaru?" Miriam, alive then, all wiry and strong asks. Watching her Annie wonders how could she ever believe Miriam was an ordinary grandma. She looked like a saucy Raquel Welch in rags. But then, who remembers Raquel Welch in rags.

She watches Nicholas acting as if he were overwhelmed by Miriam. As a child, Annie looked puzzled searching for an explanation. Her grandmother's abbreviations meant nothing. Her blank look caused Miriam to add:

"Pederast, Annie. Is he still a pederast?"

"Grandma, he cannot be anything else but what he is, and it seems that you know that already, so why ask?"

Nicholas laughs in disbelief, though something in his eyes lights up so clearly. Why hasn't she noticed it then? Annie wonders. Perhaps there is something wrong with her. Perhaps Vio further diluted her dhampire blood. Her thoughts are interrupted by her 7-year-old self-keeping up with Miriam, quite uncharacteristically.

"And how are you, grandmamma? Did you miss me?"

That was too much to take for Nicholas who starts laughing and gestures to Annie to hop in bed and embrace him.

"The nerve this child has. Just like her mother."

Content with Miriam's reaction, Annie turned completely toward her grandfather.

"And you grandpa, did you miss me?" Annie asked him having forgotten her grandmother for the moment.

"Of course, I missed you …silly putty," her grandfather said in a voice which sounded affectionate to Annie's ears, then. Now, it sounds affected.

"Let me go now and see what that animal ruckus is all about." Miriam says but does not move. Annie, finding her jovial, self-volunteered,

"Wait grandma, I'm coming to help you. What would you like me to do?" Annie replied.

"Can you repair that chair the obese policeman broke when he sat down?" She points at a broken wicker chair. "I never thought I would live the day to see a living man amassing so much meat. What's going on with the world? He was looking so appetizing as if his entire life had one single goal to be slaughtered for his meat." Annie turns to her grandfather for clues. He avoids her gaze, searching for a tissue in his pockets and failing to find it, searches under his pillow.

"I think that's more than I can do, but I guess if you give me a hammer and a few nails I could fix it." Annie walked to the very fragile chair and wondered why anybody would sit on it. "Isn't this a child's chair?" Annie asks with a crooked smiled. "Why did the policeman visit you?" Her grandfather stopped fidgeting for a moment. "Did they catch you making moonshine?"

"To inquire about your mother." Miriam parcels her words. "Apparently your mother had received an invitation to move abroad, to emigrate, and she made a request to leave the country, and give up her citizenship."

Annie looks at her grandfather uncertain that her grandmother makes any sense. "The policeman questioned us for hours if we could afford to take care of you in case Tifaru approved his spouse's departure. Only God knows how happy I was for a moment!" Miriam persists. "But the rules are that no one is allowed to emigrate if their spouse refuses to let them go, and Tifaru apparently refused to let her go." Miriam stops to recharge. No one else is breathing "Why? Beats me," her grandmother finally adds and done, goes outside to tend to the evening chores.

Even now, decades later, Annie felt the pang of abandonment and fear she experienced back in 1977 as an ignorant kid.

"Mom, what was that all about?" Vio put her arm over her shoulders.

"All that double life wore me down and Tifaru was becoming such a burden, having just lost Gigi."

"How did you expect me to take it?"

"Either you would have come with me, then, or later, when you learned who you were." Annie turns her attention to the Radeş time-loop. Her grandpa further explains:

"You know, silly putty, I was so hopeful when the policeman told us about your mom's plans." Annie is content to listen. "I did not ask any questions, but I would have loved you to move in with us. You could have gone to school here." Annie follows Nicholas's gaze. He points to a wall. Behind the wall there is the tavern. The former tavern is now empty of customers and filled with stuff, and outside the peach orchard and further down the highway and across the highway the school. The village elementary school. It goes to 4th grade. For middle school boys and girls who would walk three villages away.

"I used your grandma's dowry to build it. A sign of gratitude to the people of this village who welcomed her."

Her grandfather stops. He looks at Annie perhaps to gauge the effect of his words. Annie mistakes the pause for a dry mouth and hands him the cup of water sitting on the table. It has his dentures in it. She is outraged. Nicholas laughs. Almost too loud. It comes across as bitter.

"How much did grandpa Nicholas know?" Annie finds herself back in her University office. Each time her concentration breaks or new questions creep in she cannot stay in the time loop. She has to return.

"He was very smart, kiddo. So smart, it all took me by surprise."

"Let's go and read the commemorative plaque together. It makes me so proud of your grandma, Silly Putty." Nicholas's voice calls Annie back so powerfully, she is shaken. "You should be proud of your grandma too, especially of how much she had to go through before she could settle down here."

Annie listens carefully.

"They came here from Moldova," Nicholas starts in a shaky voice.

"I thought grandma was German or something."

Nicholas laughs. Again. It sounds menacing.

"They did not speak any German." "Of German heritage."

"Okay, silly putty, anything you say." Annie smiles.

"Shall we go and read the commemoration plate on the school building?"

Annie springs to get him the cane, but surprisingly, he does not need it. Annie does not mention it. They get out of the house. The church's bell tolls.

"Except for this priest, all the priests in this village came from my family, the Radeş."

"Is this your family village?" Annie asks as if the thought has just come to her mind.

"Yes. It's ours," Nicholas adds and sits down at the big wood table under the walnut. "Bring some peaches to eat, silly putty."

"That's why grandma chose to stay with you. You could protect her." Annie says when she comes back and lays the ripened fruit in front of their eyes, much to her and Nicholas's surprise.

"Why are you saying that?" His voice sounds foreboding.

"I don't know. I guess because men protect women? Did I say something wrong?"

"No, silly. I was just amazed you seemed to know so much," and perhaps catching himself, "It wasn't that your grandma was persecuted. It was that she was pregnant, unmarried, and her parents looked suspicious, as if trying to send her off. Especially that they ran away. They disappeared. But she was saved with us, the Radeş."

"Was mom going to leave without me?" Annie's seven-year old mind seems preoccupied with other thoughts.

"Silly Putty Face, I saw no invitation. Maybe this was all made up by that very fat man." Nicholas carefully cuts each peach so precisely as if he were a neurosurgeon.

"Where was she trying to go?" Annie presses further stretching her thin arm to get a slice. Nicholas nods, implying she has to wait for him to finish his job. "Grandpa, your hands are not shaky any more. You have recovered so well."

"Germany," he finally whispers in an effort to seem not well. Annie smiles as if she caught him. "Or something like that."

Annie has an epiphany. Her jeans! Her mom must have received a package recently. She is on the verge of losing concentration and return to 2016 New York. She wants to stay longer with her grandpa. While fighting her contradictory desires she hears Nicholas's monologue while cutting the peaches. The smell is intoxicating.

"Miriam's grandfather had been chased out from burg to burg because he could not control his appetite. Apparently, despite being married he loved local peasant girls, and though no one saw anything improper other than a slap or a wink, a girl here, a girl there started to disappear, wherever they stopped to make a living. He defended himself by implying that he was the victim of national xenophobia, but each time the accusations surfaced, Miriam's family had to move. Luckily, they learned about an estranged Romanian landlord, who was spending the summer at Baden Baden, and needed someone to take care of his vast Romanian estate, located somewhere in a place called Moldova. And this is how Miriam's parents became land administrators at a time of much want. They administered a vast estate located in Moldova. In exchange for the ability to settle and work, they had to pay a large sum of money every year, a sum negotiated every seven years. When the time came to renegotiate the sublease of the land, they met their farming tenants in a town hall meeting. The farmers first listened in their humble, obedient manner, and then, they shouted and threatened. While the farmers needed the land to survive, they could not accept the proposed sublease because it put them in too much dependence on the weather. That summer they had a dreadful drought. Another year of drought and they would starve. There was only one way out, if their word had no weight. They would revolt. When the meeting broke down, Miriam's dad went home wearily. He was afraid of how his family would react if they were attacked in the middle of the night. They would be afraid, feel cornered, and perhaps fight back. The tenants set the elders' house on fire. Villagers called your grandma's family names and they had to flee."

Annie laughs. The seven-year old finds a moment of respite:

"Gramps, are you pulling a grumps on me? Who flees for being called names? They must have fled for having done something awful. Do you know kids call me the kike's daughter? I'm a communist's daughter. Daddy Tifaru, no matter what grandma Miriam says is a communist, isn't he?"

"They called your grandma's family parasites! Imagine being called blood- sucking vampires!" Nicholas ignores her.

"Miriam's dad was not a parasite. The landowners who employed him were the parasites. Grandma's family worked. They administered the estate and oversaw the bartering and enabled the economy of the land." Annie adds and feels the need to applaud herself for her little speech.

Her grandfather has turned to the water pump. He fills his hand with cold fresh water and splashes it on his face. He then brings a handful of water to his mouth to drink. When he is done, Vio's socialite laugh breaks her concentration again.

It is the evening of May 17th, 1909. Vio, like all other Parisians is in attendance at Châtelet. Except her, who keeps attending the premier, no one else has ever dreamed of seeing anything like what they will soon experience. Pavillon d'Armide, Festin and Prince Igor are on the program. As soon as the bells in the hallway ring, the house lights start to dim and people stop talking as if under a spell. Vio, with her then companion, a late-comer who rushes in, amid half-breathed apologies. The Russian composer, Tcherepnin appears from under the stage and stepping on the podium with his baton ready, acknowledges the public perfunctorily with a nod. He begins the opening strains of his own Pavillon, and Vio disappears behind the curtains knowing that something magical is going to happen. Without any guidance she finds Vatsa's dressing room. It displayed the greatest possible order. She noticed the costumes already hung up and prepared. His dancing shoes were lined up in one row on the floor. On his dressing table, in military precision was set out his make-up – sticks of Leichner grease paint, from the darkest to the lightest. Bakst was just finishing there with his professional advice, and the hairdresser was affixing his wig and head-dress with glue, so that no leaps could dislodge it. The wardrobe mistress was inspecting his costume to see if anything needed a needle or thread. Diaghileff was shown in by Vassy, Vaslav's personal bodyguard, to make sure everything was just impeccable. And then as Vaslav appeared on the stage, the instant he began to dance his first variation, a murmur went through the public. Diaghileff materialized himself on the very seat next to Vio and she was terrified thinking that her cover was about to be blown. Luckily the audience burst into an unceasing storm of applause after Vaslav's first tour en l'air. There were resounding cries for "Encore, bis, bis, bis," when Diaghileff faced Vio:

"Why are you here?"

"You cannot touch Stravinsky." "Stravinsky who?"

At that time Igor Stravinsky is not within Diaghileff's radar. But Vio does not let that detail get in the way. "Actually, you have done enough harm as it is with Vatsa. You could have used protection. Now, you cannot touch anybody else."

"Am I blacklisted?"

Vio stands up and added her voice to the increasing chorus of "Encore." Despite the rigid rules of the ballet which forbid any artist to appear on the stage and bask in the audience's adoration, Vaslav returns and makes eye contact with Vio. He smiles at her timidly and then bows and retreats.

Vio looks at Sergey Pavlovich Diaghileff:

"Sacha, isn't it? Why don't you bring everybody to my soiree tomorrow night? It's the penthouse of my private hotel, Dacia."

Annie witnesses her mother dominating a Dhampir as powerful as Diaghileff. She feels giddy. Proud. The 1909 stand-off could have been re-written as many times as her mother chose to re-live it. Still. Annie experiences it as the first time. Until she doesn't. She is taken aback by memories.

"Kiddo, where are you going?"

"I'm not sure. I must have missed something important the first way around."

And it hits her as soon as she says it.

"Peach picking. Miriam, did you say peach picking?

"The peach trees are such melancholy plants. Never too tall and their fruit so bouncy and juicy."

"Miriam, Nicholas cut peaches for me. I can see him. He cut his finger by accident and I shivered. I wanted to run home to get him a band aid. He said it was no big deal and he sucked his cut finger."

Annie stops talking. She's back in Radeş, sitting at the table with Nicholas sucking his index finger.

"No need to go home. It will stop by itself." With his intense blue eyes pinning her down, Nicholas hands Annie a slice of peach. Annie refuses it.

"It has blood on it."

"Who was killed by a drop of blood?" Nicholas shows his shiny denture.

"No one," Annie says and bites it.

"No, don't do it," Vio and Miriam can be heard. Only too late. They were not there then. Annie sees herself slightly bending in discomfort.

"Who was Nicholas?" Annie's question is met with silence. "Who was Nicholas? Why did he want me to ingest his blood?"

Applauses. Riveting applauses interrupt Annie's close breakdown. Paris is enthralled with the Ballets Russes. Wherever Sasha goes, Parisians stop whatever they do to congratulate him. For having discovered Nijinsky.

***

6 CHASING LIFE

In a whirlwind, Annie feels pulled back in a different direction. The wind of remembrance blows to Podunk, 1982.

Taller and with two long braided tails she sits at her kitchen table. A blue jumper slightly worn-out, indicates that this is not her first year of middle school uniforms. She often forgets to change or better said, she never changes if her mother has friends over. She has nothing to change into except pajamas.

Laughs are coming through the opened window from her living room where her mom entertains and from outside. The Chemistry textbook is opened to the Mendeleev Table. She needs to memorize it for the next day's test. She reads it once and she remembers it. Color, composition and position of each element on the table. She is chewing her pencil and aware as she puts it down. No signs of feebleness. You make yourself into whatever you want to be, Annie the 12-year old repeats her new mantra. The second time she finds herself distracted ready to chew her pencil, she stands up and opens the window as widely as possible.

The poplars are so big and green. The sun is kept at bay by their thick foliage. She recognizes Mia's hearty laughing and stops daydreaming. Other voices can be heard. Annie becomes curious. She stretches on her tiptoes and pushes half her body out the window. Mia and her posse of three other neighbors play cards, probably Crazy Eights, Annie's favorite card game, on the orange bench. Each bench had its color. Mia came up with this idea and because she bought the paint, the bench became hers. Sort of. Lost in spying, Annie mechanically grabs a piece of apple. Her mom always provides an entire Jonagold apple sliced on a plate. Annie chews it silently, forgetting she is spying. In plain view, she stares blankly in awe.

Mia, by chance or not, notices Annie hanging out there with half her body outside the kitchen window. She alerts her friends to look up. Embarrassed, Annie retreats from the window, squatting on the floor.

Emboldened by Annie's apparent meekness, Mia and her friends start chanting, "Annie, we see you," until Vio goes out on the terrace and admonishes them to be quiet, or else.

"You are likely to disturb Annie, who does her homework in the kitchen."

"No, she's at the window, looking at us," Mia replies.

"So, be quiet. Your screaming must have interrupted her concentration." Vio retorts. A lioness when her daughter needed public defense, she turns toward her own friends who cheer for her.

Still squatting, Annie is too embarrassed to be proud of her mom coming so swiftly to her defense. Assured that Mia won't reply, and that the conversation has ended, Annie returns to the table. She is ready to start her Math assignment, when giggles from the orange bench reach her. The easygoing Mia and her friends, Kaitlin, Sandy and Lauren, are having a great time. And none is an A+ student. Not one.

Kaitlin lives on the floor below hers, and is two years Annie's senior. Years earlier Annie had to beg her mom, Kaitlin's fourth grade teacher then,

"Mom, if Kaitlin repeats the grade no one ever will talk to me again," Annie reasoned.

"Annie, Kaitlin can barely read and she has a ways to go before she knows the multiplication table."

"I don't think Kaitlin will ever need to know the multiplication table," Annie continued undeterred.

"You are right. She excels at calligraphy. I keep telling her that she would have had a great future as a copyist in a XII century monastery."

Annie smiles at that memory. It warms her little heart up whenever envy is close to deter her from enjoying her days. Kaitlin is not the only older friend of Mia's. Sandy is a high school student, and she does not mind wasting time playing Crazy Eighths.

"Go away creep," Annie hears Sandy's voice. She cannot help herself and stands up. It is Robert, Sandy's twin brother. As Annie stretches to see what is going on, Robert looks up and smiles. Annie sits down. It is too late. She has broken her concentration. She's out of her Podunk, 1982, time loop.

"Mom, are you anywhere around?" Annie calls out from New York. "Mom, that was Nicholas's grimace. That was not a 15- year old high school boy's smile. It was menacing. Robert had no reason to make that face at me."

Vio opens her time loop. She is on the beach in Venice.

"Mom, for Christ's sake, really? Don't you ever fear anything? How much vampire blood do you have in you? Aren't you afraid of getting fried?"

Vio, smiling, turns a parasol in her gloved hands, shoots a smile at her daughter, who for the first time sees in her mom what probably both Paris and Venice have already: "the face that launch'd a thousand ships / And burnt the topless towers of Ilium?" It's early evening. The sun is far away from zenith. How did that glowing face stay so hidden in Podunk? Reminded of her birthplace, Annie retraces the afternoon her memory has picked for her to parcel. Robert is gone. Sandy, too. Mia remains sit between Kaitlin and Lauren, as she always does with nowhere to go. The rumor mill says Mia's home is off limits while her father is at work: her mom uses it for her neighbors' pleasure. So, Lauren, the "optician's girl," because she lives with Gary, Podunk's optician and twice Lauren's age, has become Mia's mother figure, and a public housing celebrity. Most men smile at her with renewed youthfulness. Women can only hope Lauren will not respond to those smiles with a home visit.

"Mia followed Lauren's advice on getting her own Garry." The inevitable happened one day.

"Why would anybody want a bold, spectacled, man-toad?" Annie replied.

"That's not the point, Annie."

"What is the point, mom?" Annie replied when Vio brought up the subject.

"The principal rounded up all the teachers and inquired whether we had any additional knowledge. Mia picked Dan, and kissed it. I mean kissed him there."

"Where?" Annie finally asked though she was not curious. Any kiss involving Dan was painful to her ears.

"Never mind, Annie. The point is that Mia did it and the older boys locked her up in the bathroom to kiss theirs too, because theirs were bigger than Dan's. And the county school inspector came and we had the meeting. No one was fired. Mia was brave enough to acknowledge her tutorial took place in Lauren's home."

Annie remembers how she swallowed a few times; she could not talk for a few minutes.

"We are talking about Dan whose father is the morgue director, correct?"

"Annie, why are you reliving this old, unpleasant event?" Vio inquires as her friend Marchesa Casat introduces her to d'Annunzio.

Vio cannot understand a work. Vatsa started some commotion. La Marchesa implores her to go and see what is wrong with Vatsa, which Vio does. He is naked, save a pair of shorts and blood is pouring out of his left nostril. He needs a doctor, Vio tells Sasha who helps Vatsa lie down on a chaise long. The henchman, as Vio calls Vatsa's bodyguard, makes sure a beach umbrella gives him enough shade. Vio, knowing that Vatsa's condition will only slowly aggravate, chooses not to press on the issue of a doctor's help.

Ignored, Annie finds solace in her memory. With all that misery, being almost 12 has its benefits. From the kitchen table, with her books open in front of her, Annie enjoys life, especially the crisp air the nearby Carpathian Mountains provide, and the blue sky. Silence is friendly. There are no whispers and no hopeful chuckles coming from the living room. Probably Tifaru is home and the guests have vanished. Conceivably, Vio's school teacher friends shyly envy her for being lucky enough to have a husband, even if they all laugh behind his back for being sexually flawed. Conceivably, again, they enjoy a man coming through the door and terminating their childish behavior. Putting an end to her guess, Tifaru opens the kitchen door, goes to the refrigerator and pulls out a bottle of plum brandy, țuică, and starts gulping the tar smelling liquid ignoring Annie until the alcohol kicks in. Then he puts the bottle back in the refrigerator and addresses her:

"Chasing life in textbooks?"

Nodding, Annie smiles and looks down. The Idiot lies open on her lap. Dostoyevsky's Idiot. And then the silence is broken. She can hear Fini's voice coming from the living room and she jumps out of her seat.

"Do you see this white spot?" asks Ms. Fini, as Annie calls the little spinster, the retired teacher, Stefania. Fini commands the attention of the couple of younger women surrounding Vio's dining table under the intimidating Tiffany chandelier they all think a kitschy fake when its noisy crystals made themselves visible.

"It must be Tifaru's from Gigi," the guests attempt to explain the-out-of-place dinosaur hanging above their heads. Tifaru's forbidden relationship with Gigi, by then finished, has reached Podunk notoriety. Rolling their eyes in disbelief they probably hope that day wouldn't be their unlucky day.

Fini reads Dina's future, but that question, Annie judges, is directed at no one in particular. Fini looks so lovely in her slightly dirty worn-out outfit, as if she has spent the entire morning getting ready for the afternoon show. Her thin receding hair, hardened by molding spray, is all rolled up and presented to the world like a plate of stuffed cabbage. The white roots woven with brown ends have less of a rejuvenating effect than advertised; Annie cannot help temporarily assessing the end result. She follows Fini's impressive bony index finger stuck inside the dirty coffee cup, surprised to notice the perfectly manicured red painted nail, which summarizes Fini's personality: frail but commanding attention.

The coffee spot is not in sight, perhaps because it does not exist or perhaps because Annie cannot see it from the open window, where she stands to avoid the mixture of perfume and flatulence which accompanies Fini. Luckily, no matter the season, the living room window remains open because Ella and Dina, Vio's colleagues, are chain- smokers.

That warm day in May, Annie mostly forgets about Fini, attracted by Mia and her two friends.

"Why don't you go outside to play with them?" Vio inquires.

"Oh, there is nothing we can talk about," Annie replies and both, Ella and Dina, are cheering her answer.

"If you say so, but to me it seems you want to be part of the world and away from it."

"Vio, Annie can do it. If anybody can have it both ways, you child, can. She has all the knowledge books can give her, and that's impressive," Ella comes to her rescue. Annie can still appreciate the jolt of Ella's support.

Vio, in a rare moment of solitude, addresses Annie bringing her back to the present,

"Annie, are you all right?" "Yes, mom. Only confused."

"Annie, humans' lives are usually less challenging than ours. I don't know what you intend to understand from all this back and forth in time and space. No one had to fight any secret desire to swallow tadpoles. No one enjoyed lying down and imagining tadpoles swimming inside their empty stomachs previously filled with water so the little creatures would enjoy their new inside pond," Vio adds and Annie agrees.

"You are right, mom. I am not trying to learn anything from humans. I am trying to get clues about myself. I cannot make sense of what I am supposed to do or not do."

"Maybe you should have spent time playing with those kids. Maybe having less time for introspection would have made you happier, what do you think?"

"Play with them in my nylon skirt and patent white shoes? You made me look so weird."

"I wonder," Miriam interferes. "So much comes from our attitude, and from how we related to the others. Yes, you could have played cards with them if you showed some interest, for instance."

Miriam ends with a strong cough, and both Annie and Vio give her time to add something else. Nothing comes.

"I found it easier to spend time with the adults," Annie explains her choice.

"How queer of you, kiddo."

"I'm sorry you were so miserable those early years," Vio comes closer to Annie almost touching her shoulders.

"You didn't seem to care then, so why care now?"

"I did."

"You appeared way too busy, and now I get it: you were busy protecting Dina, and Ella, and those kids from their imaginary friends."

"Now that's harsh, kiddo. She protected them for the likes of Gigi and Fini, and of course, the friends of Dan's parents, but that you never got."

"Fini?" And then Annie stops. It makes sense. Fini was not telling the future. She was so careful to let everybody imagine what they wanted. To Dina, her 6th grade English teacher, personable and knowledgeable, Fini let her imagine whatever she wanted. Annie's gaze remained fixed on Dina, who stared into the small and dirty cup of coffee covered by her lipstick marks. Pointing at anything in that tiny space, Fini remarked, turning toward Dina with hungry eyes:

"That's a pretty big white tent. Do you see it?"

Dina relaxed, and leaned back into the chair.

"Is that the wedding tent?" Ella intervened. Dina laughed and lit another cigarette recovering her easy-going mannerism. "Are you inviting us, or you'll be too embarrassed to show us off to your mother-in-law?"

Fini's eyes flickered for a moment. Vio stepped in between Fini and Dina holding a large plate of beignets. The only one standing, Vio added, "head over heels," and sat down, having served herself one and turning toward Annie with the plate. That final remark was followed by a unanimous murmur of approval, as everybody's mouth full with the freshly fried dough was encircled by confectioner's sugar. Annie smiled at their angelic looking faces and excused herself.

"She did not invite anybody, did she?" Annie turns towards her mother who watches Annie's memory.

"No." Vio says, and she allows Annie to see Fini devouring Dina the night Vio went to Radeş to investigate the fire: Vio arrived too late to save Miriam. There had been no wedding.

Never intrusive, only observant, ignorant of her pedigree, Annie grew up accepting the adults' addictions to the little white pills and enjoying the ritual of coffee worship. Since her tender years, Annie participated in the ritual. She would grind the coffee grains in the hand-operated copper mill. When her arms hurt, she would take a break, licking some pots and being scolded and hushed away by her mom's relaxed face and minutes later she would start anew because she wanted to be part of the afternoon ritual.

Once a week, sometime between four and five in the afternoon, perhaps after a brief nap at the end of a demanding morning of teaching, Ella, and Dina, her mom's colleagues and friends, came by for a cup of coffee and a moment of joy. Vio always baked or fried or assembled some dessert to greet them. Sometimes, babka or Russian coffee cake, or fried beignets "exactly as Tennessee Williams liked them," Vio would introduce her dessert and no one doubted the veracity of that amazing detail though it sounded as if she had met the man himself, which must have been a figure of speech, undoubtedly they thought. Most often, Vio served crepes filled with home- made jams.

"How did you manage to make the jam? You were never home."

"This tells you how selectively distorted your memories are. I cooked for you, didn't I? I worked as a teacher in Podunk and my afternoons were filled with extra work, correct? So, my dear child, you just have to accept that I excel at time management."

Annie resigns herself that she will never get anything more out of her mother. She focuses on the late spring afternoon she has happened to fall upon in her search for meaning.

There she is happy to eat her mom's beignet. They are so crunchy and sweet. Vio brings up more coffee and pours it in another set of fresh small cups.

"Vio, you really know how to make coffee the way the Turks served it when they owned the land," Ella the historian adds sipping carefully. "It is the Turkish coffee pot, the copper ibrik, that makes the difference."

Watching her teachers transforming from overworked and tired beings into chatting butterflies bubbling with things to say, once the boiling pots of hot coffee are sipped, has transfixed Annie for years, and made her understand that conquerors do bring civilization to the people they occupy, and it is only just for history to record their deeds in indented paragraphs.

Ella and Dina reach real joy when Fini reads their future. With her penchant for telling women what they want to hear, Fini gets love in return she can easily exploit. Once, with Dina, when Vio was not watching. Otherwise, in séances of tasseography Fini tells them about dreams of everlasting happiness. Her readings of unspoken hope are made manifest in coffee grounds. The random arrangement of the coffee drippings inside the little cup turned upside down, after the muddy liquid has been almost sipped entirely, Fini translates into an "imminent marriage proposal," or "a romantic night," or a "fantastic vacation."

Unmarried, Ella and Dina seem more like overgrown silly siblings, as if adopted by Annie's mom for the mere fact she has her own apartment decorated with both a husband and a kid.

"For years I had admired your ability to have friends, mom," Annie turns to Vio. "I never made friends."

"My child, friendship requires sharing intimacy or at least hosting your friends so they could confide privately," Vio almost caresses Annie's hair.

"You never shared your secrets," Annie stops her mom.

"Vio did share secrets."

"How come Fini did not divulge who you were?"

"She couldn't. Though a step above Tifaru, she was no Dhampir, "Miriam interjected.

"Fini too had been dhampir prey?"

"Yes, and no. Both Tifaru and Fini had once known love by another name, having caused the demise of a dhampir, and thus, their own lives, but their punishment was to outlive their dhampir protectors."

"The dhampir bite does not give its victim immortality, only a tedious death sentence for all to see and avoid." Miriam explains the obvious. Annie imagines she knows it all too well from her own grandpa Nicholas story and his epileptic-like spells.

Lev, never too far from Vio, surprises everybody coming to Venice.

"Sasha, dearest, I got your cable."

"Oh, sending the money would have been enough," Sasha replies when Lev comes to embrace him. Everybody is delighted.

"The more the merrier." Someone says squeezing Vio's hand, but Vio does not pay attention to such trifle of attention. She does not remember if Lev was supposed to join them or not, but she admits she is content. Happy almost.

***

7 SUMMERTIME AND BUBBLEGUM POP

After their Parisian success, Diaghileff chooses to bring Nijinsky, his dearest prize of the moment, to his favorite city, Venice. There he has plans of introducing him to other dhampirs.

"I am waiting for my turn with Vatsa," is the talk of the town.

"Given that Dhiaghileff has at most a couple of years of interest in him." Venice has a way of attracting the scours and the authentically rich, if authenticity makes one more enviable. In battling for Vatsa's attention, their generosity surely surpasses their aristocratic nature. And they do flock to the Grand Hotel des Bains de Mer on the Lido. An exquisite choice.

"Vatsa is not in a good mood, is he?" Vio addresses Lev who has somehow moved next to her.

"Vatsa has been upset the entire day. He would have loved to swim in the Laguna, but Diaghileff rejected the suggestion."

"Sasha could have asked someone else to take him to the beach because he cannot stand the sun."

"Instead, Sasha took him to the Accademia and the Scuola di San Rocco."

"Always on the look to find ways to refines his pray," Vio beckons and takes a sip of champagne.

"Unexpectedly, Vatsa had a sudden coup de foudre for an unremarkable visitor,"

"And Sasha got jealous?"

"No, according to Sasha, Vatsa attacked the man who ignored the overture, almost biting him," Lev adds with a smile.

"Poor Vatsa."

"And to top it all, he had an epileptic seizure when they went to their room."

Dhiaghileff bit his ear very delicately, and he finally stopped only to end up in an epileptic seizure, Vio summarizes the situation. Aloud she says,

"So, why isn't he in bed recovering?"

"Sasha would not let him. Marchesa Casati has scheduled this soiree to celebrate Vatsa. No one can miss it."

La Marchesa makes her entrance leading a black panther on a chain. Her smile is hideous.

"She seems in a bad mood herself," Vio comments.

"She definitely needs entertainment," Lev agrees. And the entertainment escalates with Vatsa sitting between Gabriele D'Annunzio and Isadora Duncan, and stomping his feet faster and louder with every passing moment.

"Pray, dance some for me," Gabriele commands, "I want the Dieu de la Danse to dance just for me."

"Pray, impregnate me," Isadora cannot let some else's impertinence shadow hers.

Vatsa is standing, his eyes red with barely suppressed anger. Diaghileff smiles like a magician disregarding the nonsense. Vio feels a pang. The same Annie feels from her end of the time loop. Experiencing the eerie pain of humiliation Vatsa suffers. For a moment, Annie is taken by the scene and momentarily wonders if her yearning to understand is the consequence of her lovelorn character. She blurts it out,

"How come Vatsa, whose language knowledge is limited to Russian, understands those commands in Italian?" Annie asks no one, "Both D'Annunzio and Duncan spoke Italian to him."

She could add that it is proof of Vatsa metamorphosing under the influence of Sasha's bites in unexpected ways.

"You float when on the stage. You hardly touch the ground executing the most technically difficult steps without any effort. The New York Times reports that you can stop in mid jump." D'Annunzio declaims. "Do it right now just for me. I pray you."

"Vatsa, you are the god of harmony and beauty," Isadora interrupts the author in an effort to avoid being undone. "For me the number of pirouettes and entre chats are no longer as important as the harmony of movement. You can do anything acrobatic you imagine. You are the god of dance. Pray give me a baby."

The hostess, as if having lost her mind, joins in the chorus of acclaim.

"Vatsa, indeed, your phenomenal upward thrust is magical. Your extra strength in the toes and the metatarsals makes experts understand how in the allegro pas you do not come down completely on the balls of your feet, but barely touch the floor with the tips of your toes to take the force for the next jump. You magically use only the strength of the toes and not the customary preparation with both feet firmly on the floor, taking the force from a deep plié. Vatsa, do pray marry me."

Vatsa won't stop stomping his feet. He stands up. Sasha does the same thing. Only he laughs, and his confident, charismatic laugh distracts the guests from noticing Vatsa's strength. With one hand Vatsa has just picked up D'Annunzio, lifting him up, ready to hurl him out the window and was getting ready to do the same thing with Isadora Duncan who was getting undressed as if to help the lifting process. Sasha, possessing equal strength, reaches the dancer's place in a jump and pushes down on Vatsa's arm. Vatsa's eyes suddenly clear. He sits down properly like a chided student. He puts down D'Annunzio, who has no idea of what just happened; thinking himself too inebriated. Isadora applauds.

"How brilliant. Vatsa, you are a born choreographer."

Turning to Sacha, "when will we see Vatsa's own dances?" And the discussion takes a tamer route.

Vio feels safe enough to catch up with her daughter. She searches her in her Columbia University office. Annie looks half asleep reliving her memories. Vio understands Annie is back in Podunk. It takes her no time to find Annie's journey, to July, 1984.

Annie makes lunch for Tifaru and herself. She seems adroit at chopping cucumbers, tomatoes, parsley and green onions in small but equally shaped cubes. She does it so fast the knife becomes a moving image rather than an object. And she stops. To look at her cut. She pinched the radial artery of her left index finger. Blood springs out everywhere. Tifaru opens the kitchen door. She instinctively puts her wound in her mouth, licks it, and takes it out. She continues chopping. Slowly. There is no sign of her wound. It closed up.

"That's a huge salad," he says opening the refrigerator and taking his brandy.

"It's our lunch. Unless you want an omelet, too."

"No. That should be enough. Thanks. You did not need to work so hard. Especially that now you are part of the 28 club," he continues. "Take this time without your mom around to chill. Go to the movies." He stops drinking and takes two tens out of his pocket. Wrinkled and dirty, they don't sit well on the table sprinkled with blood, which Tifaru, by then using reading glasses, does not see.

Annie blushes with pleasure. She took the entrance exam to Podunk High School's gifted and talented section with a concentration on Physics and Math. The high school admission test lasted two days - the first day covered pre-Algebra and Geometry topics, and the subsequent one was devoted to Romanian grammar and literature. It was a big deal. She had swallowed so many butterflies in the weeks waiting for the results. To push away the pain Gabe called dismissingly, "butterflies in your stomach."

"By the way, I love your butterflies' memory." Miriam interjects.

Each year, hundreds of students would take it but only the first twenty-eight would be selected to be bestowed with the additional education needed to pass the exit high school exam, the baccalaureate, and the college admission test four years from then. Anybody who made it into the 28 club became college-bound, with a good chance to make it into another club, The Intellectuals'. Though the Party acted as if they were despised, they were much in demand. On their narrow, un-athletic shoulders rested the burden of growing submissive, but entertaining, and predictably supportive, of the Party.

"It will be ready in a few minutes," Annie adds when she notices a small slice of her finger on the blade. There is no gap in the index now. She quickly takes it and puts it in her jean's back pocket. She notices how slender she's become. Then she licks the bloody knife clean. The gesture amazes her. A Hindu Yogi lying down on a bed of spikes.

In Venice, Vio relishes the small break. A welcome respite comes when Reinhardt, Countess d'Orsay, Debussy, and Vollmoller join in for coffee and after meal drinks. Vatsa has retired quietly, and smiles in a corner. Diaghileff cannot take his eyes off Reinhardt, as he keeps calling Nijinsky a "genius" and the "greatest miracle ever." He suspects mockery. Vio calms down Reinhardt with a lighthearted kiss.

"And your enviable position among mortals still eluded you. You know, Annie, I will never understand how this was possible."

"Mom, did you ever lick your own wounds?"

"No," Vio replies and as soon as the word resonates in her ears she realizes its meaning. "What was going on with you?"

"Changing, I guess."

"Without being aware of the changes," Annie replies, and too uncomfortable to bring her thought to an end she reverts to Latin. Annie starts whispering conjugation of Latin verbs.

"What are you doing?"

"I learned Latin that summer. I memorized the full conjugation of 304 verbs waiting to hear whether I had made it in the G&T high school program or no. That's "amare."

"A what?" Miriam interferes.

"Nothing mom. Annie learned Latin during the two weeks I was away at my summer resort, in Paris, as we now know."

Annie starts mechanically,

"Present tense: amo - I love, I do love, I am loving; imperfect: amabam - I loved, I did love, I was loving, I used to love; future: amabo - I shall love, I am going to love, I am about to love; perfect: amavi - I loved, I have loved; pluperfect: amaveram - I had loved; and finally, future perfect: amavero -I shall have loved.

"Sic transit gloria mundi." Miriam's voice interrupts the craziness. "What on earth are you doing Annie?"

The Latin utterance has the effect of shaking up Tifaru. He turns to Annie translating it with unexpected inflection:

"Thus, goes the glory of this world." Then, he sat asks, "What made you say that, Annie? Gigi loved that phrase. I always thought it a password. It gave him entrance to places I never thought existed. Strange.

Gabe rings their apartment bell, ending any potential conversation. After the exams, they have spent most of the time together while waiting for the high school G&T program entrance results. Some mornings they would go to the nearby river. Annie could not stand the sun, and she was never big on swimming. Sometimes they would only watch the fish swim by and joke about catching them. Annie tried once and surprised herself and Gabe when she was successful. Gabe blushed because he failed, and went for a swim. Quite a bad idea: The dam built upstream opened accidently and the tumultuous waters carried Gabe away like a small trunk. He was making matters worse as he started to be very agitated. Providentially, his head hit a rock, and Annie could rescue his floating fainted body when it got caught in the branches of a fallen tree. She placed him securely on the river bank.

Annie smiles at Gabe opening the door.

"What's up old man?" She asks and

gives him a kiss on the cheek. "Come in. I will make an omelet for the two of you," she ushers him in as Tifaru puts his head through the kitchen open door.

"Come in Gabe. I need company to celebrate your success."

"Hello, Mr. Tifaru. Annie did an impressive job. Perfect scores in both Math and Literature. You must be one proud dad. I know mine would like to be in your shoes."

Annie's smile broadens. When the two-week wait period ended, Gabe ran to tell her she topped the admission list.

Coming in, Annie pushes him to the living room table. It is clean. She brings in the dishes and the salad bowl. She keeps the door open as she beats the eggs for a fluffy omelet, her specialty.

"Mr. Tifaru, can Annie come with me to a dance?"

"Are you inviting me to a dance? Why?" Annie comes in holding a spatula in her hand.

"Annie, stop asking that many questions. Of course, Annie is coming with you, Gabe," Tifaru answers for her, "You have reached a milestone, Annie. That's why."

"I have nothing to wear," Annie complains dividing the omelet between Gabe and Tifaru, and serving herself with some salad and a scrumptious slice of whole-wheat bread.

"If you eat like a sparrow, you may still fit in your 5th grade clothes," Gabe laughs speaking with his mouth full.

"Manners, my little man. Watch your manners or this one will forget about you," Tifaru points out Gabe's savage table manners.

"You gave me an idea. Mom has an amazing silk skirt in a nice orange shade matching my chestnut hair, and light beige crepe shirt which she never wore, saying that her body changed after my birth. I am going to try them on and you'll tell me if I look weird or not."

Barely 95 pounds at her 5'3, Annie was light as a feather and quick on her feet. She's ready to go, when she sees a pair of new sandals her mom never wore. She tries them on. Perfect fit. She looks at herself in the mirror and blushes. She is beautiful. Now she can let herself be seen by Gabe.

As she goes to the living room, Gabe catches sight of her first.

"Wow! You are so beautiful Annie," he says loudly and covers Nicholas's whispered warning:

"Remember the kiss. It only takes a kiss."

Gabe and Annie laugh. Tifaru raises the bottle of plum brandy and toasts for "smart youth."

"Did you hear his voice, then?" Vio opens her time loop to Annie's.

"Apparently, not then. Why did he warn me then again?"

"Where was the dance?" "Gabe did not say."

The memory Annie enjoys moves forward in the day. She sees herself holding Gabe's arm on their way to their classmate Collin's house, Dan's best friend.

"That's why she chose this memory. It must have Dan around," Myriam interjects.

"Jean, Collin's cousin, will probably be without a girlfriend. If you like him, you can dance with him. I don't mind it. I will do the same if I find another girl. We know each other forever." Gabe keeps chatting nonstop.

Silently, Annie squeezes Gabe's hand.

Letting themselves into Collin's home, they notice the cousins and their guests talking animatedly about the music playing as background noise. Annie finds that funny. Abba's sound fills in the space as they arrived.

When "Knowing you Knowing me" ends, Collin approaches them and introduces her to his cousin, Jean. Annie nods. Dan never makes it to the dance. Instead Jean, a rising senior in some town some twenty miles away from Podunk, Collin's cousin, proves to be the main attraction. As the sun sets, Jean must have seen something through Annie's skirt and shirt because he knocks at her door next day to ask her out for a stroll in town. Walking her outside the building brings a huge smile to Annie's face and nail biting to Mia, who sits on the bench gossiping with Sandy.

"Hey, Annie," Sandy greets her a bit louder than usual and Mia bites her nail a bit too hard perhaps because an "Ouch" is heard by the passing couple.

Jean is three years older than Annie, and living in Ploiesti, some thirty miles away, adds further lure to his senior high school status clutter: he may and indeed does write her letters.

He has great penmanship. He writes long letters in very legible hand writing. He loves to describe her appearance in as many ways as possible, and Annie enjoys reading about herself. The mail comes in the afternoon and Annie experiences high hopes and low despair in the course of each morning that her boyfriend might have forgotten her.

Perhaps the most interesting part of their fortnight-long relationship is that Jean failed to be utterly average due to his remarkable physique. Nothing mediocre there. He is truly and most noticeably repugnant: short, bow-legged, already balding, with a complexion sporting the marks of chicken pox, and his eyes two different shades of green. This colorful element adds a je ne sais quoi distinction to his entire appearance, in the way a limp or even a prosthetic could add dreadfulness to a merely unpleasant body. His ugliness helps Annie reconsider old stereotypes: men are from Mars and women from Venus. Jean comes from a toad's rear, but that thought has not yet occurred to Annie. It will, though.

The couple of walks around the town Annie and Jean take change her local status: she suddenly become beautiful in the public perception. Similarly, because he is able to walk with a girl in touching distance, Jean becomes more than the nephew of Collin's parents, both successful local doctors. He becomes a catch, too.

This mutual benefit does not escape Annie's bright mind, and she realizes that many unions between a man and a woman exist on joint assistance, a kind of symbiosis, rather than shared feelings of love or something approaching love. She wonders about her parents' mutual benefit.

"You are tedious, my dear Annie. When is this going to end?" Vio stops this recollection.

The end comes on a Friday afternoon. The postman delivers the mail from Ploieşti to the 2A mailbox. It is addressed to Annie Tifaru, in very cursive letters. As expected, it is from Jean.

The letter, naturally, starts, in Romanian with the day, time, and hour when Jean put his fountain pen on the piece of paper. Jean loves his electronic watch,

Annie knows. The time marked is "14:53:7." Under the time, it contains the typical "Dear Annie," but then it continues with the exceptional "I hope this letter finds you and your family in good health because I have some very urgent though unhappy news to dispatch to you." To cap it all, it carries on in English:

Knowing me, knowing you There is nothing we can do Knowing me, knowing you

We just have to face it, this time we're through

Breaking up is never easy, I know but I have to go

Knowing me, knowing you.

Then, rather in an abrupt way it reverts to Romanian, only to end, "With gratitude for your time, Jean."

"The toad," Annie finally gets her imagination together and refers to him employing a descriptive label, "had the nerve to choose English as the language of breaking up," despite him being a Romanian through and through!

"His choice is neither British nor American English, but in the spirit of early globalization, he has selected Swedish English!" Vio sounds mesmerized.

Annie remembers the song she danced to when he first saw through her skirt at that ill-fated party.

"Annie, you needed to know how to handle boys with a kiss. That's an invaluable life lesson which comes with practice."

"The kiss."

"Kisses darling. Embraces. Hugs. All of them. There is no recipe. You move from one to the other and more as the moment makes you feel."

"Instead I ran into my bedroom and started my Catullus therapy," Annie remembers her reaction to the letter and starts reciting.

> *Vivamus, mea Lesbia, atque amemus,*
> *rumoresque senum severiorum omnes unius aestimemus*
> *assis.*

"Let's live, my Lesbia, also love," Catullus 5.

"At least it focuses on vivamus." Vio sighs and blows some smoke in perfect little circles above Sasha's head--to his exasperation.

***

□

8 WHAT A WASTE!

Vio continued to be an absentee mom for the rest of the 1984 summer, Annie remembers and resentment takes over her. A pang in her heart and a Young Communist song reminds her about her struggle to become a perfect New Human Being, then defined as the New Man. She turns on her computer and starts typing. It was the sunset of an era no one but Tifaru still believed in. No tunnels or factories or dams were being built. People were eager to take their chance with time and wait on lines for the end. As she types, absorbed in her reminiscence, Annie ignores the time loop Vio opens hastily because Lev is still in her bed, naked and only half asleep. Vio sips her morning Turkish coffee and elegantly smokes her cigarette. She coughs lightly trying to get Annie's attention.

"I've lost track of your summers. Do you still attend to your digestive problems somewhere in Transylvania?" Her daughter engages Vio without facing her.

"Why ask now, Annie?" Lev turns and kisses Vio's silky knee tenderly.

"Don't know. My walk down memory lane reminded me of the New Man. I really loved that concept. The fights against capitalism, which I did not know what it meant except that I was a princess and the ogre needed to be kept at bay."

"So, we're not done with Podunk?"

"Mom, the answer is in my past. I am going there, and it may seem a bit meandering. If it bothers you, by all means, don't stick around. This life is not worth living. I have to anchor and have no direction."

"Kiddo, don't be so harsh with your mama. You only have one mama."

"And one dad, but guess what. I don't know what I cannot have. Mom, care to share that with me? Is it a vampire? A dhampire or worse?"

"Most likely a vampire, so you aren't missing much," Miriam made herself heard.

Annie, still dismissive of her mom and grandma, returns her attention to her teen years and their Podunk apartment.

It is a summer Sunday in 1984, and Tifaru is all dressed up in "construction work clothes," going to the lot where for the last five years he has worked hard at building the foundation of a two-story brick home. Annie has remained ambivalent always thinking about the Three Little Pigs and their travails to escape the Big Bad Wolf.

It is noon or noonish. Vio did not believe in telling the time exactly so there is no clock in their apartment. Both Tifaru and Annie are quietly eating at the kitchen table. They share an omelet smiling tolerantly when they happen to make eye contact. Annie reads The Brothers Karamazov, where Fyodor Pavlovich has the kitchen built outside the main house, into a cottage because he does not like the kitchen smells. Thinking about "kitchen smells," Annie takes a break and looks pensively at Tifaru who uses a knife and a fork to eat his omelet and chews his small bites without apparent interest in the food itself, only in creating a protective cushion between his stomach and the brandy.

"What were you thinking, Annie?" Vio asks looking freshly made up. Lev is tying a knot but Annie is oblivious to the Parisian scene developing in her mom's boudoir.

"Probably at Tifaru and his laughable bourgeois dream to move out of our socialist bunker, the public apartment building where we have been living. The communist dream of a single-family home." Annie sounds derisive as she types ahead still ignorant of her mom's affairs.

"It was supposed to be a beautiful brownstone, and remember, it was just across the street from your princess Zazou."

"More like a brown brick house, wouldn't you say?" Miriam interferes jocularly.

'Mom," Vio addressed Miriam, "can't you find anything better to do?"

"In the graveyard in Radeş? Have you been there recently?"

"It was a good dream, Annie," Vio ignored her mom's disruption. "Having a villa to move our family away from the grotesque public housing setting worked as a sufficiently strong bond for us and it was for most people. Unfortunately, few could afford it."

"Weren't we lucky Tifaru won that piece of land at poker?" Annie stops typing remembering something only she knows. "He was so happy when it happened. He too dreaded the gossip and the intrusion and the forced intimacy with people no one wanted to know or like. I guess you two had a lot in common, mom."

In her remembrance, Tifaru, in his rugged jeans and old linen shirt, is acting as if caught in a spider web. He wants to talk to Annie, but then he doesn't. Perhaps taking pity on him, Annie stands up and closes the window and turns on the radio to listen to Voice of America the radio station broadcasting music and news and stuff which otherwise would have been unreachable to people behind the Iron curtain. Tifaru is unsure about her motivations and is getting tenser. In his HR informer position he is not supposed to listen to such subversive radio stations.

"Now, we can talk without anybody listening to us. They will be too scared having to report eavesdropping to Voice of America," teenage Annie approaches Tifaru.

Tifaru goes to the refrigerator, takes his bottle of plum brandy and pours himself a glass. He drinks it without a word.

"Daddy Tifaru, I made it in the high school G&T class, and with me you made it."

"Yes, you did it, Annie. I cannot thank you enough."

"Not a big deal."

"Annie, you will be in the same class with the offspring of lawyers, doctors, and other Podunk success stories. Annie, I wish Uncle Gigi was here. He would have been so proud of us."

Annie notices how uncomfortable her teenage self was at the moment. For the young Annie could not imagine the people Tifaru has just listed being important, even if they would act graciously, tolerating his nocturnal presence around them. That young Annie could not comprehend what it meant that they played poker as a means to inform on each other, and that in daylight they remained the best of the system while he, Tifaru, remained a loser, a pederast, an outlier. But in 1984 Annie succeeded and Tifaru had become their equal, only better: he would be a G&T class parent, exactly as they were, but they would all know that Annie had succeeded on her own. Much like their hush-hushed conspiratorial winks and laughs behind his back hurt him, now he could look into their faces and read their pain. Annie, his daughter whom no one dared to hurt, would make it out of Podunk. The Party could not ignore such a Brainiac.

"Let's talk about some more important issues. How are you today?" Annie asks Tifaru.

"I am happy the wait period is over. I could not take the pressure much longer, Annie," he finally laments, and adds: "Thank you, Annie. You are a good kid." She touches his head playfully. His hair is still thick and curly.

"At one point he must have looked a bit like Cassius Clay, but very briefly, because his inner Peter Lorre must have taken over," adult Annie remarks while typing in her Columbia University office.

"He did look very attractive." Vio agrees. "Not to me, of course," she quickly adds as Lev jokingly pouts pulling her down under the covers. They start giggling like adolescents.

Annie ignores everything going on in Paris. In her Podunk 1984 memory, she finishes lunch. Tifaru is done eating too. She closes The Brothers Karamazov, cleans the table and quickly kisses him tenderly on his cheek.

"Wow, look who likes pervs," Miriam's voice could be heard in the background.

Tifaru turns toward Annie and almost cracks a smile, as if he knew that success comes to those who share it.

"Where were you last night?"

It takes Annie a moment to realize that Tifaru actually has asked her a question which could have been answered by more than a "yes," or "no".

"Where were you last night," Tifaru repeats himself in a paternal voice that startles them both.

"Collin had a victory party," Annie responds standing with the book under her arm indicating she would rather go to her bedroom.

"Really?" Tifaru continues standing up and getting glass of tap water, something Annie has never witnessed before.

"Is that strange?" Annie replies in what seems to be a well-rehearsed manner of avoiding adults' questions.

He nods a "yes," and loudly adds "Collin? Is his dad the director of the general hospital?"

"Yes," Annie confirms and looks at Tifaru surprised at his sudden interest in her life. Then, Tifaru nods a bit more and leaves the kitchen mumbling something which is far more familiar and comforting to Annie than the preceding conversation.

"What did you two do for the rest of the summer?"

"I really don't know. I will have to see and go through each memory."

And her memories roll in front of her eyes. One day Tifaru brings home a library book, in addition to the stolen notebooks. Annie reads the title aloud "The Capital. Vol. 1."

"Daddy Tifaru, Marx? This is as rebellious as I can imagine," Annie comments running to her bedroom to read the book. What a change Marx would make in their lives. Annie puts down her summer books and devours Marx's book, its historical data, arguments, and many fast-drawn conclusions. She starts looking forward to Tifaru coming home from work: he commutes by factory bus, so they can talk. They discover that they enjoy each other's company more than expected or imagined possible. In a moment of supreme paternal confidence, Tifaru asks Annie whether she would like to learn poker, but Annie declines.

"It's a waste of time."

Maybe Annie does not need society like her mother does, addictively, as if it were a drug. Or maybe Annie does not expect her words to hurt Tifaru. While she utters it, she trembles understanding it is the answer her grandfather gave her when she first asked him to teach her chess. Annie repeats word for word her grandfather's reply when she tells Tifaru:

"It's a waste of time."

"Why did you say that?" Vio asks her. "Nicholas said it after he gave me the

chess set, don't you remember?" Vio shakes her head negatively. "Yes, after he produced his gift, the chess board game, I asked him whether he would like to teach me and he caressed my soft strawberry blond hair for a long time before refusing. I didn't take no for an answer and eventually he played with me once or twice. I remember now, he added, 'You have spark Annie, and sometimes that's all you need in life.'."

"You did have spark, but not all the time. Oh, Annie, did I hurt you that badly?"

"It's too late to lament mom, let's see if I can learn something more from my exquisite 1984 summer."

"You did exhale every time you excelled. I am so proud of you, Annie."

Gabe has taught her how to play chess during the 1984 summer. When the weather is too sunny for Annie to go outside, or they feel too lonely to enjoy reading on their own, they get together and played.

That is the summer when Tifaru and Annie become chess pals, too. Tifaru, probably happy that Annie has inducted him in the selective club of G&T parents, works hard enough to build the foundation of their future villa, on the lot across the street from Annie's princess. In that dark and cool cement structure, Annie learns to love reading in the hammock Tifaru sets up for her. The rooms above are taking shape, one wall after another, as she read about labor and value and added value. When Tifaru builds four walls he calls it a room and covers them with the foundation for the next floor. They talk about what to label the new headquarters, and Annie comes up with the brilliant idea, "the kitchen." Tifaru does not need any persuasion. The following day he brings with him an old table and two small chairs discarded in the street, and furnishes their new chess quarters. For that short summer, Tifaru and Annie enjoy each other company almost as much as when she was unsure whether the egg, or the chicken came first.

The historic Abba mail from Ploiesti was left in the public housing mailbox while they were playing chess. The postman saw Annie and thinking he would do her a favor said "Annie, you have mail from Ploiesti!" Annie ran to the fence to have the news repeated, while Tifaru called back "check and mate."

"You know you cheated," Annie says and runs to their apartment to get the mail.

"You are so wrong, Annie. I never cheat. I make blunders, but I do not cheat." Tifaru adds but Annie is long gone downstairs, only to reaper somehow smaller and thinner, and altogether different.

***

9 LEADERSHIP CAMP

Perhaps the nascent relationship between Tifaru and Annie would have blossomed even more, hadn't her new high school sent Annie as their representative to the Youth Communist Leadership Camp of 1984.

"I still love merit rewards," Annie hears herself.

"You had no merit to point to in that high school when you go to two weeks of

camp paid by the Party." Vio announces with such aplomb, that Miriam interferes.

"Kiddo, you surely have reason to like merit-based examinations."

"Granny, I am so happy someone understands me."

"Kiddo, we all understand you. The problem is that you are on never-ending flux."

"Shht, granny. I want to hear what happened to me then."

The leadership camp was in Sinaia, not far away from Podunk. Without a car, or because they did not really have money, her family did not offer to bring her there.

Annie has visited only those places her school decided pioneers needed to visit: the prison where their president spent his truant youth, or the dam which brought them electricity.

That is her first time visiting the fabled royal ski resort of Romania's former kings. Indeed, it is summer, but Annie easily imagines the trail and touches the same trees they must have avoided carefully on skis. At least both the royals and Annie have shared the same gaze at nature. But the best attraction is the camp itself.

The camp's grounds belong to one of the few boarding high schools in 1980s Romania, the very military high school the royals built in an attempt to produce a military class in Romania. Its campus is as big as Annie's hometown, she believes. Annie is so childishly excited she could not wait to return and describe it to her now best friend, her life tutor, Princess Zazou, always respectful, witty, and so tolerant of her dreams.

Soon after she arrives, she is directed to the dorms. The rooms are huge and segregated by gender. Her bed is to the right of Simona's bed. Simona is a rising senior from another high school in her county whose future was all mapped out for her. Annie thinks that she has either passed the law school entrance exam next year or she would marry her beau and his amazing gala apple orchard, one of the most fecund in the county. To her left side there is the wall separating the girls' bedroom from the boys'.

Classes on leadership are scheduled each morning immediately after breakfast and the wake-up jog around the campus. Then they have lunch and the afternoon classes in history and one hour to prep for the final show of entertainment, music and dance. The dinner and another hour to get ready for the night round up the daily program.

During leadership classes everybody has to express their views about improving their high school's graduation rate or recycling efforts. Annie mentions incentives, such as free camps to those at risk of failing graduation in case of success and rewards for recycling. The instructor seems skeptical, but a skinny dark looking boy with curly hair nodded every time she speaks and takes notes. Annie notes him and mistakenly thinks he is the mysterious flower sender. In a way no one would describe becoming, Annie smiles at him on an average of every other day.

Thankfully, the leadership class ends as any hour-long class would end. Next, Annie goes to history. Those classes focus on so many details from the pre-historical era that Annie expects to learn about the imminent excavation of a homo romanius, but that never happens. Lots of attention is given to the Middle Ages, the darkest period in some histories, but a highlight in Romanian history, because the Romanians became the very outpost of European Christianity on the eastern front, blocking Asian invaders of other persuasions from reaching further west.

Too bad they could not play that role before the Roman Empire had been destroyed by the barbarian migrators, Annie thought, but she never expressed that reflection aloud, and her choice proved wise. Otherwise she could have been perceived as too critical of the Romanian people, as her friend Simona was when she asked why everybody assumed that being Orthodox was somehow better or superior to being Catholic. "Shht!" almost everybody roared. "The Pope was Catholic" the skinny young man noticed, and Simona added, "and he still is," as a requiem for her participation during those classes.

The main attraction of the camp is the talent show. During the prep sessions for the final show, the dark looking skinny boy, Annie hears referred to as the Duke, a rising senior at a prep-military academy in Bucharest. Nevertheless, the role of leader is taken and then everybody else gets a role on a team and a specific task. Annie is separated from Simona, and chosen for the Duke's team, The Quasar, a winning name, Annie thought, right again. The Quasars' main task as a team was to write the sketch, the funny critical play for the final show, and then come up with a theme song and choreography. The Duke's chosen girlfriend, the representative of another famous boarding school, Bucharest Ballet High School, Diana, was charged with the winning choreography.

Annie, maybe because she has no idea what a military prep academy is or maybe because she does not care, devotes herself to the ballet, and soon afterwards to shooting with Duke. For lack of competition, most likely, she writes the sketch overnight. She brings it to Duke, who suggests they start another prep round in a couple of hours. They do. The Duke seems impressed with her command of details and especially with her penchant for learning English quotes from the English version of Marx's book.

"Why are you doing this? It is obvious you have not suffered since the regime changed, and I doubt you are here to do anything."

"I was invited, and I count the ad-hoc performer to be my friend. Please, do not harm him."

The Duke did not reply. He continues his training. Annie is a natural. His hand is shaking. Hers is steady.

When the talent show is finalized, Diana offers to teach Annie the basic positions in ballet. Diana has Russian intuition. Annie's ballet will never go further outside than her beautiful mind. But in 1984, nothing needs to change. Annie laughs when asked about her previous ballet experience,

"I was quite good in gymnastics," Annie boasts by way of explanation. "But I bet you cannot do this," Diana retorts lifting her right leg 180 degrees upward from her left leg. "Can you do a back flip?" Annie replies, doing it.

"Girls, that's enough." The Duke ends their bickering when a crowd forms around the dueling gals. "Why don't you both perform during the final show?" And they quickly agree.

The Duke takes Diana's hand and retires to some room. Simona takes Annie for a walk. "Are you okay, Annie?" Simona asks.

"No."

"Annie, that pompous son of the bitch keeps notes on everybody," Simona shares her discovery.

"I don't really care what that means. I love shooting with him."

"Annie, you are not just a gal taking orders and shooting targets."

"I don't see anything wrong being that gal, Simona."

"He is testing you. He wants to know what you think so he can make his notes about you." Annie rolls her eyes. Undeterred, Simona adds, "The guy is so full of himself he cannot be less interested in anybody else. You are falling for him."

Annie could not believe her ears. "Simona, I really don't see why any of this is of interest to you." The former girlfriends part as if they never met.

The following day the Duke approaches Annie and tells her that he has found the sketch excellent the way it is and he is going to give it to the actors he has designated appropriate for the parts, so Annie was free to take some gardening classes during rehearsals.

"What about more shooting?" Annie replies taking the Duke by surprise. He has not expected that.

"I have not made any reservations."

"The cemetery is perfect. Its tombstones could not be better practice for us. Don't you think so?"

The night is splendid. The details ravishing. The Duke comes with two Kalashnikovs. Annie does not ask why. She seems content with anything the Duke does.

"Have you ever exhumed a corpse?" Annie asks and the questions disturbs both of them.

"Young communists do not engage in such depraved acts," the Duke replies, and Annie feels proud of him. She has made up her mind. She feels happy. A Caesar in control of the situation.

"Of course not. But it would be fun. Imagine exhuming a fresh corpse still full of blood."

The Duke is visibly shaken. He fails to take his notebook and write his observations there. He starts wiping.

"Annie, who are you?"

"You just said my name. I am Annie.

Let's shoot."

The Duke is in no shape to start shooting. His hands are shaking. His hearing fails him too. He hears bursts of laughing.

"Are you laughing at me, Annie?"

"Why would I do such a foolish thing? I like you very much. You should be laughing at me. You don't like me."

"I like you, Annie."

"Oh, no. But that's not relevant now. Right now, we are going to shoot. You are going to shoot at me and I will bite you if you miss me. It sounds fair. What do you think?"

The moment those words are uttered, Annie stands up. She is all shaking and sweating.

"Mom, what happened?"

Vio and Lev are both stunned trying to make sense of what they have inadvertently witnessed in Annie's memory trance.

"Forget about it, Annie. It happened such a long time ago."

"Mom, obviously that moron did not shoot me."

"Obviously."

"Did I devour him?"

"So, that's how the nightmare started," Miriam mumbles. Lev hears her, but Vio is too troubled with Annie's vision to hear anything else.

***

10 POETIC JUSTICE

With fall 1984, Annie's morning routine changes for the first time in 9 years. Until then, Annie would follow her mom to school, as if she were Vio's puppy. In high school, classes start 30 minutes earlier. Also, Podunk's High School was built on an orchard at the outskirts of the town, in the opposite direction from her previous epicenter of public education. Instead of the ten- minute waddling walk, Annie has to walk briskly twice that speed and twice that time to start her daily instruction.

Walking to and from high school, Annie has three choices. Each one is dictated by her company or better said, her lack of it. She strolls along the river bank when Gabe walks with her. She strides along the main street when she is late for class. Her favorite route is wandering along the small street where Princess Zazou lives.

"Annie loves that street," Vio shares her memories with Miriam.

"Yes, that schmuck of Tifaru was really lucky when he got that piece of land right across from Zazou's headquarters."

"I would not go that far, Zazou was Zazou, but Annie was taken with her."

"It looked like a spell."

"It could have been," Vio agrees with a yawn.

"Vio, if you were a bit more conscientious as a mom we would not have to sneak for a preview of Annie's memory to understand what the heck is going on with that girl."

Vio giggles. She and Lev are having fun. Miriam closes her loop with Paris keeping open only her connection with Annie and her Podunk. Annie is following a meandering stream of memory. Here she is like a little awkward six-year-old kid filled with mysterious desires, knocking at the door of Princess Zazou's attic for her weekly English classes. She adores when her princess uses her sea shell collection housed in a shoe box to teach her how to count in English up to 120. Now she jumps years later when she still did not know the identity of the two beautifully curly children who had stared at her while learning English for almost a decade. Her question is more how they succeeded in staying still until the presumed artist finished painting them, rather than their real names.

Vio laughs remembering also Annie's recollection about their annual picture taking session. Tifaru used to take them to Podunk's only photographer who arranged them differently but always sporting flip flops and dark sunglasses, in front of a Hawaiian cardboard set. "Don't move," was what the photographer said instead of "smile," or "cheese."

Annie wonders why they stopped taking those quaint pictures. A memory reel comes to her. In it, Tifaru defends his rebelliousness explaining he is saving money for their new villa. At the sound of the word "villa," Vio agrees with the budgetary decision. Annie hears herself saying, "Don't you make enough at poker?" Everything turns black in her memory film. Then after a few moments another film starts.

Perhaps due to its proximity to where her princess lived, across the street, Annie sees herself visiting Tifaru as he builds their house foundation. Tifaru and a few other men, hired help, seem very handy with mortar and bricks. Annie sits in her hammock or on the grass and reads. If she were lucky, her princess passed by and Annie waved to her. For years Annie and her princess talked about how they would become neighbors and Annie would stop by to say good morning and she would reply very ceremoniously, "good morning to you, too, your young highness."

In another film Annie sees herself daydreaming about Tifaru winning big at poker and those moments when she did not know how to thank her nameless gods. Her princess never made any judgmental observations. Suffice it to say that she had seen Tifaru working in the garden and those times a little gentle man often stopped by and they both talked for hours. Annie would nod. Eventually, everything reached a standstill. Annie stopped hoping they would ever move there. The cellar always full with her mom's winter preserves was the only indication living people were connected to the place. Otherwise it looked like the ruins of a long-abandoned dwelling.

By the time Annie reached high school, she lost any sense of imminent change. Marching to high school along the street where her princess lived and her family villa refused to appear, Annie was pulled apart by the happy memories the house next to her lot held and the dissatisfaction with the barren lot of land across.

"I am getting dizzy with all this free stream of memory association," Vio complains buttering a piece of toast.

Annie's memory is back to Fall 1984. It is a wet, cold morning, and Annie is happily reciting poetry on her way to high school.

"Finally, she is expressing herself."

"Finally, the kid is showing some feelings."

"Poetry is Annie's way to express her feelings. She loves memorizing and reciting poetry." Both Miriam and Vio stand still. Annie is reciting.

High school
Cemetery of my youth
Pedantic professors and pathetic exams
Even today I quiver when I hear
High school
Cemetery of my youth!

***

"Annie never forgets and never forgives."

"I guess you are right mom. Her coming-of-age broken heart was marked by taking up poetry."

"It's that Jean boy. Annie never forgave Jean for using Abba's lyrics to convey the bad news. Do we know what happened to him?"

"Oh, I don't think anybody saw him in Podunk afterwards. I never asked."

"Take a look at this fast-forwarding movie."

Annie writes notebooks upon notebooks of original poetry: words conveying betrayal and sadness and duplicity and perfidy, or worse, treachery. With high school, life opens its limitless options to Annie. She joins the poetry club.

"Yes, I remember the high school poetry club. It took a lot of time out of Annie's hands. The teacher running it wrote poetry himself and better yet, he looked like a poet, too. He had curly, long, unwashed hair and thin almost translucent hands with long, unevenly cut, dirty nails. The dirty Lucien de Rubempré, Annie referred to him, because his name was Lucien and, like Balzac's character, he was very charismatic and mysterious about his true love affairs."

"Shht, let's listen what Annie remembers," Miriam encourages Vio to stop her own reminiscence.

"Annie, I like your writing. You have a unique voice," he tells her the following day after she read another doomed poem and ran out when done to avoid both applause and eventual criticism. "I will choose something and submit it to a literary magazine on your behalf," Dr. Lucien continues.

Annie is so thrilled. Lucien Radu is a doctor in literature, a matchless achievement for a Podunk teacher. He earned his PhD with a dissertation on Catullus whose poem 85 was one of Annie's favorites.

Odi et amo. quare id faciam, fortasse requiris?
nescio, sed fieri sentio et excrucior.

Her memory moves forward to the next year. Annie's ID sewn on her jumper identifies her as a sophomore. It's a

Wednesday club meeting. Dr. Lucien asks her to stay after the club meeting ends.

Annie is trying her hand at sad but hopeful love lyrics.

She recites one of her more optimistic poems. All in attendance stand up and applaud. Among them stands up the high school stallion, Leo. He is smiling at her. She is happy.

"The child is happy."

"Finally. Let's keep her with this recollection. Poor soul."

Annie spends a lot of time thinking about how to reconcile the trappings of love and volatility, with her inborn distrust of vacillation.

"Open yourself up to love," Dr. Lucien tells Annie one day on the dark windowless hallways of the Podunk high school.

He hands her a pocket size little literary journal, opened at a page containing a small poem by Annie Tifaru, "Adolescent Love:"

I hate and I love.

Perhaps you ask why I do this?

I do not know, Mother, but I feel it happen and I am torn apart, Father.

"This is Catullus 85," Annie spits out the words without catching their meaning.

"You're wrong," her mentor cuts her short. As Annie is preparing to reply, he quickly adds,

"It is similar, but no one is aware of it." Dr. Lucien smiles. Annie keeps staring first at the paper then at him, her eyes retracing the movements of a pendulum. "I like suspense. You may win the competition," he tallies her chances.

"Only very bad poets steal other's work without crediting it." Annie finally breaks her silence.

"No. It is taking what is for the public to take. It is recycling." He smiles again.

"It's stealing. Nowhere does it say Catullus is the author." Neither does Annie know nor want to relent.

"First, the lyrics are in Romanian, not Latin. Then, there

are multiple differences. Finally, without Annie Tifaru's help, Catullus would have been forever lost." Dr. Lucien replies leaving her holding the journal. "Look how they ignore me, a Catullus expert," he adds a polite afterthought meant as an encouragement.

"I will tell everybody it is Catullus," she whispers fighting a strong impulse to scream. Dr. Lucien turns and smiles, "You cannot do such a thing. You are the communist leader of all Podunk high school students. The party would be very upset if you acknowledged deceit. Even worse perhaps you would imply that the judges are a bunch of idiots who had no idea of Catullus or any other great poet. Which one would it be?"

And for the first time she has the sensation of déjà vu. Not of Dr. Lucien, the teacher, but of the real Dr. Lucien. Her teeth clench involuntarily as her palms curl into tight fists. She knows him viscerally. He has no fear because he is not a mere teacher. He is much more. But for the first time Annie rises to the challenge. She has stopped smoking in public so no one would judge her weak and vulnerable. But she is neither. She approaches him her eyes incandescent. She hisses. Nothing she has heard leaves her mind. It's inaudible for her classmates.

"You may be found unfit to stand any college exam," Dr. Lucien continues and his silk dark outfit smells of tobacco and

…blood. His face has a sliver of dirt on it. Hardened blood. Annie is not even an inch away from his face. He looks scared. "Why don't you calm down and wait? Next month the winners of the national poetry competition will be announced. I doubt you will win. It is not a patriotic poem. As we both know, Catullus was into Lesbia, not into Rome."

Vio stands up in full uproar. Lev is holding her hand.

"Mom, what was that?" But Miriam is quiet. Annie's vision is not over.

The times passes by. It is Spring 1985. The end of Annie's first year in high school. Dr. Lucien's premonition proves right. Annie does not win the first prize. She wins the fourth prize – or what the committee identified as the prize of encouragement for the most promising poem by a first-time submitter. Dr. Lucien goes to the ceremony alone, and takes Annie's prize with a pompous speech on behalf of all the students of Podunk high school, and the few recently departed via freakish accidents.

The event is televised. Surrounded by Ella, Fini and Dina, Vio watches the ceremony. Annie comes out of the shower right when the ceremony is over.

"Oh, Annie, Dr. Lucien just finished reading your poem and I am so impressed. It is so mature."

"It is marvelous, my child. We are all so proud of you."

"Annie, who's your inspiration?" Fini asks with a wink she soon regrets.

"Aunt Fini, so many poets. I don't know where I should start. I feel them all on my veins."

Annie has a strange feeling of running away. She does not need to prove herself. Yet, she does not know what she needs to prove. It is all new to her. Her power. Her desire to push back when pushed. They all turn away from her and congratulate Vio for having such a talented daughter. Annie smiles, forgotten. Still she excuses herself. She needs to walk or vomit. She dresses up as quickly as possible unable to choose which one she would settle for next.

"Silly Putty. Don't be rushed. There is time for everything," Nicholas' voice can be heard. "Princess Zazou is expecting you."

"What?" Vio exclaims in disbelief. "Mom, where are you? We need to talk. When did this all happen to Annie?"

Miriam is quiet. Vio finds herself alone. Lev is gone. Just her silver cigarette holder, and a bottle of champagne. Taittinger, her favorite.

"Damn it. Damn it all."

Outside her apartment building, Annie sprints by the four neighbors playing Crazy Eights on the bench in the courtyard. Mia's look is envious but guarded. Annie has a destination. She doesn't. They both mumble a fast "hi."

Annie then salutes politely the older women sitting in the sun on the other bench in the communal courtyard. As soon as she is out of their view she is ready to run. She feels so light she can easily fly. She settles for running, but she does it so fast, she goes unnoticed.

"Take it easy, Silly Putty. Take it easy."

Annie stops in front of the street where Tifaru works after hours to build a house, and her princess lives. "I am no criminal," Annie tells herself as she gets ready to leave the chestnut boulevard, and enter the quiet street which holds so many dreams of hers.

"Annie," a voice interrupts her thoughts and her decisions. Annie's head turns in disbelief. It's a classmate. Dandy, his nickname, because he tries so hard to be above his given status--the son of a shoeless peasant. Annie looks at her watch. It's late. He has missed the bus which takes all the students living in the neighboring villages home after school. For some reason, Annie looks worried. She does not want to face any more transformations. "Annie, I saw Dr. Lucien on TV accepting your prize for poetry." He adds. Shit, Annie tells herself. Her palms are curling into tight firsts. She has to stop it. She holds her breath. Her fists unfold. She has to think fast. Dandy is the second brightest in her year. If someone could have conceivably read Catullus, it is him. "I liked your poem." He keeps talking. Annie continues to hold her breath and assess the situation. She is pretty sure Dandy does not know any Latin. How sure is she? Pretty sure. When she sent the inquiry about creating a Latin Enthusiasts Club, no one responded to her posting. Also, coming from the village nearby Podunk, he has been exposed only to Russian in school.

"Thanks. I have to go though." Annie finally inhales, and then exhales. She has to keep it loose.

"May I accompany you?"

"Why would you do such a thing?" Annie replies a tad too fast. Dandy is taken aback. He shows it taking a step back and bowing, letting her go. His smiles look impudent. The more she thinks about it the surer she is that he is outright impertinent. He is going to blackmail her. Her fists are tight. She is taking a step in his direction.

She is ready to start hissing and her eyes radiate a laser beam-like stare.

"Not now, Silly Putty. Not now. You know you can. Not now." The voice of Nicholas whispers in her ear.

"I would rather go alone, if you don't mind" Annie finally replies, unclear how she has found the strength in her to deescalate.

"Of course, I totally understand. I would do the same." Dandy adds and somehow as an afterthought he hands her a notebook similar to hers only filled with his poetry. One poem starts with,

"How good to have you/ What a miracle to have me / Two different songs, hitting and mixing and kissing…/"

Annie cannot believe her eyes "This is not your poetry," she blurts out.

"I don't write poetry, Annie. I'm not like you. I copied poems I like most for you." Dandy explains himself. "Let me know which one catches your fancy." A car stops by and he jumps in. Then he pulls down the window and asks. "Would you like a ride? This is my dad. He's an engineer." And he pulls up the window as the driver turned to face Annie.

"Gigi?" Annie blurts out. It cannot be, and then he looks so much alike.

"Mom, did you hear that? It cannot be Gigi. Can it? You helped me make sure he was gone. Am I losing my mind? Mom, answer me!"

Miriam is quiet.

In her spring of 1985 memory, Annie remains dumbfounded in the middle of the side walk. She seems unable to figure out what is going on. She closes Dandy's notebook. She has to know what he knows. As if plagiarism is not enough a plague, the potential blackmail compounds the situation. She needs advice. And quickly. Luckily the advice resides with Princess Zazou.

"Dandy or Dan, who is it going to be, Annie?" Vio has inserted herself in Annie's memory. Lev watches her in disbelief. Vampires can easily do it, but dhampires risk the wrath of their employers if found out.

"Mom, I am so happy you are here. Actually, what are you doing here, aren't you supposed to be with your friends?"

Vio looks around. She is dressed in her fancy Parisian clothes. She has to get out fast.

"Yes, we were having so much fun. I was trying some new clothes Fini brought to have us buy. I thought I would take a walk and see how people responded to this crazy fashion."

"You are so beautiful, mom. Buy them. If you can afford."

"Oh. Come home maybe Fini has something for you too."

"I cannot mom. I am in trouble and I was going to talk about it with princess Zazou."

"Talk to me. I saw Dandy talking to you earlier. What's in your hands?"

Thinking about Dandy makes her skin crawl while thinking about Dan gives her shivers.

"Dandy copied poems for me."

"How thoughtful. I guess Dan is history if you have accepted Dandy's gift."

"I don't think so."

"Annie, I think I can help. You have cast Dan as the unreachable prince and Dandy cannot be but a valet or perhaps worse."

"Mom,"

"Annie, this is no Strindberg's Miss Julie."

Annie feels excruciated. Her mom is

right. This is no play. But what if she can fix all her fears with a kiss.

"Annie, are you all right?" She is standing in front of her princess who was trying to get in but Annie is blocking her way. Annie looks around. Her mom is nowhere in sight.

"Did you want to see me? Come in," her princess adds.

Annie follows her. The princess occupies the attic in a rather spacious three-story building. The attic is a huge dark loft with an unfinished terrace at one end inviting falling accidents and a spacious room at the other. They choose to sit on the wicker armchairs on the terrace.

"What a beautiful afternoon," the princess starts. Annie smiles. She is at a loss. She does not know how much she should divulge to her princess. "I heard that your poem won the teenage prize of promise," the princess continues, inviting Annie to say why she came. Annie searches her face for clues. Annie loves her white denture, or what looks like a perfect white denture and her coiffed white hair and especially her always powdered face. Everything looks exactly as she has expected. Finally, Annie relaxes.

"That's why I'm here," Annie finally dares to talk. The princess waits patiently. "That's not my poem. Dr. Lucien in a revenge mood, I guess, submitted a slightly changed translation of Catullus 85 under my name." The princess starts reciting,

"I hate and I love. Perhaps you ask why I do this? I do not know, but I feel it happen and I am torn apart."

"I told him I would not keep his secret but he frightened me with terrible consequences, so I implicitly acquiesced to his game by keeping quiet." Annie talks faster and faster. "And a few minutes ago, this boy, Dandy, approached me and gave me his poems. I believe he knows about the lie, and I don't know what to do," Annie finishes in a whisper and hands her princess Dandy's notebook.

"A collection of poems. Love poems," her princess notes after reading some of the poems.

"He copied these poems." Annie explains.

"And you are afraid he's trying to give you a message." The princess does not seem convinced. "I think he likes you and he finally got his courage to tell you that in the form of his very thoughtful gift." Annie is distressed and she must have looked the part. "But you don't like him. I remember. You like boys who keep you under their radar. Funny. This is a persistent young man, and he reminds me, Annie, of a younger man I knew many decades ago."

Vio is finally relaxing next to Lev. No one has seen her. She can continue her life as before. She listens to Annie's memory almost enchanted.

"I was not married then, and I was visiting family in Greece. He was excitingly naïve and brave and handsome. And maybe uncouth at times, but so determined to ... He followed me home, near Galati, not too far from the Danube Delta. He only had himself. No money. No connections. He was self- educated, a school dropout. I was very reluctant, but I never regretted letting him in my life." Annie looks at her princess baffled. She has never shared anything about her princess life, and those reminiscences intimidate Annie.

"Now, you are a different person." Annie can feel her eyes searching for approval. Annie stands still looking down at an ant crawling aimlessly on the terrace. "I find this young man, Dandy, fascinating, but you don't think him sufficiently interesting. Could that be because he seems in love with you?" Annie continues to be startled. "I doubt that my speech will change your feelings, and I somehow doubt that this young man would settle for anything less than your true feelings." Hearing her words Annie fears the worse. "And, if you wonder about your options to buy his silence, that's why you're here, aren't you? I believe you do not know him."

Her princess smiles revealing her denture in a non-threatening, friendly way. Her anxiety is diminishing. More than advice Annie is searching to share her pain, her internal hell, to have its magnitude exposed without having to suffer any defamation. She is content that it all has been exposed. She does not have the strength to go after Dandy, to entice him with her friendship.

"Often, yes, don't be surprised, often it takes time to develop feelings. Are you willing to give this boy time?" Princess Zazou continues. Annie looks confused. "Of course, at your age there is no need to torture yourself," she adds patting Annie's shoulder.

Rain drops start falling everywhere, indiscriminately. Her princess stands up. It is time for Annie to leave. She happily excuses herself and runs down the spiral staircase outside.

Outside she stops running. She is in no hurry to go anyway. She strolls on the path approaching the shabby fence separating the street from the home her princess has made for her in Podunk, away from her native Moldova. She would have hired her grandfather's family a century earlier to take care of her feudal lands, Annie thinks and this new thought engrosses her enough to start a new daydream about the Fishers and the Zazous.

"Annie," her princess calls after her. Annie stops and looks up. Her friend's head is sticking out of the singularly beautiful bay window, perhaps the only one in Podunk. "You forgot this notebook." Annie turns and goes under the window lifting her hands. Her Princess throws it.

"Read it!" she adds before retreating inside and pulling down the drapes.

***

11 THE PREDICTABLE ICARUS

"All adolescents, like all happy families, resemble each other regardless of their gender or species."

"All they want is a broken heart, theirs or someone else's."

"I don't know if that's what I had in mind my sweet Mashenka," Lev calls Vio by her given name, Maria, only with a lover's affection.

Vio gets stuck in a project she likes, like her after-party for the 1909 Parisian debut of the Ballets Russes, for a while. Luckily Lev has kept her company with the dedication humans who just got married usually show to spending their honeymoon in a hotel room as if it were one eternal wedding night.

In New York, one ocean and one century away from her mamma, Annie too seems to have taken a break from the day to day reality. She is stuck in her adolescence. Moving forward, but not very fast.

"Oh, I remember that young man. What was his name?" Vio participates in Annie's memory call. "Leo. Almost like yours, my darling." Vio adds, and leans on Lev; both are now staring into Annie's journey through Podunk.

Annie trips and Leo catches her. Women passing by sigh with disappointment. Why not them? Maybe next time when they go to the post office to pay their phone bills, Leo's mom will ask him to take care of them. Or when they need a plumber, Leo's dad will ask him to tag along. When has Leo started his revolution? No one could pinpoint exactly, but it was certainly within the last two years, when he reached 6 feet. No Romanian is that tall. Or very few. Until then he was nobody due to his lack of academic achievement and his invisible parents. But once Leo became that tall, single--handedly, he brought Podunk to a new level of sophistication. His lanky body with that stroll became the right mixture of mystery. His almond-like blue eyes encircled by silky sandy hair added an air of superiority many in Podunk viewed as god-like and never achievable by mere humans. His perfect complexion was only matched by the way he moved as if "he don't care, smooth as silk and cool as air."

The moment he reached 6 feet, his life opened for him and to a considerable number of ladies. He was spending his summers on the Black Sea coast making friends with every single foreign tourist in need of a girl, a boy, or a mere friend and he helped them all sell clothes, drinks, makeup, and tampax products, among other items, for a buck more than he should so he could pocket it. Back in Podunk his social standing improved with every smoke he took of long pearl-white Kent cigarettes. In the summer he matched Italian-made jeans with Italian- made sailor T-shirts. In the evening he wore linen shirts which he refused to tuck in and sported suede loafers and perfect tanning. He was rumored to speak Italian. If Podunk residents knew Rossini's Figaro, they could have imagined him singing

Leo qua, Leo la, Pronto prontissimo son come il fumine: Sono il factotum della citta. Ah, bravo Leo! Bravo, bravissimo; a te fortuna non manchera.

***

Leo was dazzling. Girls needed sunglasses to look at him and women needed to keep their hands in their purses. All women loved him, and he did respect them all. The high school principal was a woman, for instance, quite large and scary and always wearing a navy-blue suit. As a sign of respect, he never smoked nor sold cigarettes inside the school or school yard. He went right across the street from the high school building carrying an extra pack of cigarettes for the eventual male teacher who, sent by the principal, asked him to move his makeshift store 50 meters further down the road.

"I can't sir, the bell will ring in 10 minutes and my clients cannot be late for class," Leo invariably answered and patted the teacher on his back while slipping a white package of Kent cigarettes in the teacher's pocket, emptied minutes earlier just for that purpose.

Older menopausal teachers he charmed with his large loopy smile which unsettled them because they never knew whether they should report him to social services as needing guidance, or enjoy his presence. His cologne smelled better than their husbands'. His hands were so large and smooth and manicured, and he used them to snatch their heavy bags full of cabbage or potatoes or eggplants, or God knows what they would buy from the regular market.

"Ma'am, let me carry that bag of yours. It looks so heavy. It must be heavy. Look, your poor shoulders have drooped over" he would tell them with a cigarette smoking itself in the corner of his gorgeously red plump mouth. They obeyed him.

The moment Annie tripped, and Leo caught her, she suddenly became fashionable. "Hey Annie," became heard like never before.

"Now don't believe Annie was a nobody," Vio turns toward Lev. Under the silk red sheets their bodies are naked but dry. In Paris it does not seem to ever be too hot.

"She's your daughter. How can I dare to believe anything of that sort, my dearest?"

"She was the high school president of the young communists' association. There were over one thousand students in that school."

"I am sure you are good with numbers."

"Darling, stop it. I am telling you this because I don't understand where Annie is going with this reminiscence."

"You don't have a clue about your daughter, do you?"

"Nope."

Next Annie moves to Leo's 18th birthday party. It is a very modest party his mom organized to celebrate him. Leo is courteous with his mother. He brings home only the girls his mother approves of. That night there is only Annie. He has invited no other girl in fact, because that party is to make his mother happy. He is awaited somewhere else later in the evening, around 10 o'clock, he tells Annie, but because good girls could not be seen there, Leo explains, he cannot take her with him. He blows the candles on the cake his mom has baked for him, and under her gaze, he dances with Annie. One slow dance goes by, then another slow dance, and then another and he still does not want to change the CD. Smiling, he looks at his mom, who nods. He bends and kisses Annie as she dances with her eyes closed. A long, well-rehearsed, often used, winning kiss on Annie's forehead. She is much too short for him to easily bend enough. Annie's knees go soft. She knows how lucky she is to have a professional give her first kiss. Free of charge and herpes. On her forehead.

"What's wrong with your daughter, Mashenka?"

"My daughter?" Vio retorts.

Annie is in heaven. She has forgotten about past sadness and continues to dance with her eyes closed. She feels an unmistakable desire to return that kiss somewhere on his neck. Suddenly, his translucent skin barely covering his strong, desire-inducing jugular cause her to lose control of her impulses. Annie opens her eyes as Leo's mom approaches her and taps her on the shoulder: Annie is embarrassed to notice Leo is nowhere around. No one is around.

Annie looks down at her feet. That year, 1985 has been the year of the red stiletto shoes. She has had big hopes for those shoes. Annie bought them from her new best friend, her English teacher, and another pupil of Princess Zazou, Rose.

"Hey, Annie, you must have a pair of red stilettos. Do you?"

"What's that?" Annie replies, smoking a Kent her new friend left casually on the table. Rose lives with her parents, in their villa, a very enviable situation in Podunk then. Dan's parents lived in a smaller villa. Not Collins. But on their porch, surrounded by a Monet-inspired garden, smoking a long white Kent cigarette and sipping a Pepsi, Annie is very content. She is treated with respect few humans bestow on each other. Mostly they fake it when they want something.

"You can have them for only 300 lei," Rose announces as she puts the box with the shoes on the table. She sits down and opens a little bag of roasted peanuts.

"American nuts!" Annie exclaims, referring to the nuts by their popular name which distinguishes them from roasted hazelnuts, or "Turkish" nuts. Rosie smiles. She is pretty. In her late 20s, she does not show her age. She does not smoke and she likes brushing her teeth. Oh, her front teeth are fake. How strange, Annie notices and ignores it. She copies Rose to a T. Whenever she can afford it. Everything Rose wears is so special and expensive.

"So, do you want to try them on?"

"Where would I wear them?" She asks, looking at the shoes with a quizzical smile plastered over her face.

"At my birthday party," Leo says as he stops by, takes a Kent and goes inside the house, following Rose's husband, a burly mustached man, known for moving black- market goods in and out of Bucharest.

"I don't know, Rose. That's half of mom's monthly wage."

"I know, but it's a fraction of their real price. They are Italian."

Annie develops a new view the shoes, the way she looks at a copy of Andy Warhol reproductions in Rose's house: not her cup of tea.

"First try them, see how they feel on your feet, and then

we will talk money."

Annie does as told. Her cigarette is finished and her hands are suddenly free. "Walk. Let's see if you know how to walk in them." Annie starts walking. The feeling is exhilarating. She is closer to the sky. She feels much lighter. Different.

"Hey, Annie girl, you look hot. My party is on Sunday. Uh, tomorrow. Let's say 5ish?" Leo adds informally, as he goes out carrying a box, heavy by its look, to Rose's Trabant. Her husband's.

"I have some savings," Annie admits, sitting down, sipping from the room temperature Pepsi and lighting another cigarette.

"Annie, would you like a taste of something else, better?" Rose's husband materializes behind her.

"Johnny, do your drinking with Leo, leave my star student alone."

Annie does not remember if she has known his name before. Johnny, as Rose called him, is a college graduate whose job is not very clear, aside from schmoozing and selling and buying, and having people over. Now that Leo seems to live with them, it's obvious Johnny is the mastermind of Podunk's corner of the Romanian black market. Leo can now be spotted more often behind the wheel of Johnny's much envied beige Trabant, East Germany's answer to the VW Beetle as the people's car. With his thick moustache and curly dark hair presiding over a protruding stomach, a rare sign of abundance at such an early age, hovering around 30, Johnny has also been able to develop the appeal of the local public library as a youth destination. He uses its reading room as a makeshift movie theater where bootleg tapes of Bruce Lee movies play each Friday and Saturday night for the equivalent of $10 a seat. Many stand smoking outside the room intent where they interject "Ouch" or "Wow" consistently during the screening and then explaining, to those who could not see, the karate move, the amazing karate move. Rose's voice can be heard each time an actor speaks. Luckily Bruce Lee movies require little translation, but Rose's expertise solves the linguistic barrier for some between the message of the movie and the mind of the paying Podunk viewer.

"I like them," Annie says though it is only half the truth. She likes Rose's attention. Rose has music, and movies, and Rose asks her to opine on what she likes so she can extrapolate what would be popular with the crowd Annie's age, and how much her peers would be able to afford for the various tapes Johnny offers for sale. "Yes, I would like to buy them," Annie adds, because the shoes are a power token. Rose thought of her as deserving them. More importantly, Rose does not think of her as "white trash" living in the lowest public housing. She thinks she is able to purchase them.

"I hope so. How are you going to pay for them?"

"I have 150 lei I can give you today. If you can hold them for me, I could give you the rest in two weeks." Annie needs to find a way to carry the discarded metal junk pieces she saw lying around to the recycling center. That would be about 25 lei. Then she has enough newspapers for another 5 or 10 lei. She can also ask Tifaru or her mom. They won't have it. Shit.

"So, let me see you walk in those shoes, girlfriend," Leo throws his encouragement in such a way that Annie stands up and walks. "Towards me, not away from me." Annie approaches him and Leo takes her arms and pulls her closer. Annie improvises a pirouette and both Rose and Johnny applaud and whistle. Becoming more than a pusher in the overcrowded black-market field is hard, especially for Leo who lacks the pedigree. But he has a winning card up his sleeve: his largesse d'esprit with his posse and beyond. With Annie in his arms he pushes her away and Johnny lets a rock'n roll tune be heard. Annie dances marvelously. Instinctively.

"Girlfriend, you have fast feet."

"I prefer Annie. I am not your girlfriend," Annie cuts him short when their faces come closer.

"You're the boss, Annie. Rose is your friend. I am just

trying to make her my friend too. She obviously likes you."

The music stops. Annie nods, and sighs. She moves along her memories. A hot day in Fall 1985, her sophomore year and Leo's senior year. That afternoon Annie is as always, at home, studying. Or reading an improving book, or practicing elocution in front of her mirror. She only exercises, stretches, in the morning. From 6 to 6:15.

"Who is it?" she calls out from the living room when she hears a tumble and then a knock. The doors and windows are open. It is unexpectedly hot. To reach her, one needs to climb up the stairs three flights up in total darkness – there is neither electricity nor windows to make the climbing less than a purely hazardous enterprise. Only those really intent in talking to Annie would take the risk of tripping a few times. That reduces the number considerably. Gabe, probably, her classmate and neighbor.

"Leo," he announces intelligently or perhaps just proud to hear his name instead of the incomprehensible, "It's me" which everybody else prefers.

Annie opens the door and there he is: Her gorgeous non-Italian stallion. Her knees are weak so he shoves her aside walking in. He looks inside her rather modest apartment and when he spots her chandelier his face lights up:

"Are you alone?"

"Yes," she states the obvious. She is alone. Very much so.

"Your mom asked me to stop by," he added insolently, pushing her onto the couch and himself on top of her and immediately started to feel her up as if pressed for time and achievement. His hands were playing with her bodily contours and he made her proud of all the morning exercise she put into shaping it. She loved it. He was a bit matter-of-fact and chewing gum did not help ignore his lack of sentiment. Perhaps that was lucky for the two of them, because there was no kissing involved and Annie did not feel any attraction towards his jugular either.

Her mom apparently crossed paths with him in the train

station while she was taking the train to go to some who knows what in the county's largest or just only city, Burg. "I'm a good mother," Annie's mom was telling herself getting into the delayed train, "every daughter deserves an afternoon delight."

Annie and Leo continued the well- choreographed, but devoid of feelings, horizontal dance for a few more minutes.

"If you want you could visit me tomorrow morning," Leo stretched his invitation sensing that he was not going to score even if he wasted a few more minutes.

"Instead of going to school?" Annie managed to enquire flabbergasted. He did not get offended. He looked pleasantly amused, and he lit a cigarette. He did not offer any to her. Out of consideration for his budget. Annie was not smoking then, but she made a mental decision that it could make her look cool. Leo looked even more attractive smoking.

"Of course, you could come over after school, but only if you want to," he added and Annie liked that generosity of spirit: If it made her happy it made him happy, too.

Then, he got off the couch and stood up. Annie was still lying down admiring his body. Leo started tapping his food playing with his chewing gum. Annie got up and brought him to the door. When she opened the door, he leaned toward her and attempted to kiss her again, almost incestuously paternal:

"Think about it and come by only if you believe in it," Leo added, as if reciting the Kent cigarettes commercial:

If You Believe in Magic!

Annie closed the door and simultaneously smiled and blushed. She could not believe her mom started testing her. So mischievous yet so motherly her way of telling her daughter she needed to do other things in addition to reading. The more she thought about that motherly gesture, the more Annie felt moved by her devotion.

The following day came. Annie did not go to his apartment. Perhaps she had forgotten his address. Perhaps she never really knew where he lived, or perhaps Annie lost interest in doing something when she really did not feel any hunger, and for anything else daydreaming was so much safer and more satisfying. Annie did not like exposing her inner self; that was becoming obvious.

She continued to meet Leo by chance, and that was always at Rose's, where Leo became a butler of sorts: he answered the doorbell, received packages and made payments. Perhaps that work got in the way of his passing the college admission test. Perhaps that failure marked him so badly that his black-market ambitions evaporated. Or perhaps the gonorrhea he spread around Podunk to dames married to the local elite black marketeers forced his sudden departure.

One day, even Annie noticed his absence. "Have you seen Leo lately?" Annie asked Rose's husband when he opened the entrance door.

"Leo who?" Annie heard Rose's voice coming from the living room where she called her to come in. "Listen to this new album I just got," Rose invited Annie to enjoy the music and smiled at her husband who was joining them with an open package of salted peanuts and some room-temperature bottles of Pepsi.

Annie thought Leo's smile had been stamped onto Rose's face, and getting ready to comment on that observation, she got distracted. Both the peanuts she was silently chewing and the lyrics of Cohen's Famous Blue Raincoat got in the way of her own words.

She sends her regards.
And what can I tell you my brother, my killer
What can I possibly say?
I guess that I miss you, I guess I forgive you
I'm glad you stood in my way.

***

Cohen's poetry, primal but inherently unthreatening, perfectly matched the salted coat of the roasted peanuts Rose also served. That discovery made Annie feel relaxed and very comfortable, and with her oblivious validation,

Leonard Cohen's voice was, in its own way, throughout Podunk, ready to soothe mildly unsettled spirits for only $5 a tape.

***

12 TAKE ONE

"We cannot stay here much longer. Your handlers will soon learn that you are not doing your work."

"Actually, I am doing my work. I am keeping close tabs on the most dangerous mole of all times, Prince Myshkin himself," Vio adds and jumps out of the bed pursued by the prince himself.

"I am dangerous my little Mashenka.

Wait until I catch up with you."

Vio turns in mid jump to see if indeed the prince would catch up with her. He does. And as time stands still, Vio finally understands Lev has no trace of dhampir. His flesh is neither pink nor weak. He does not need the blood of any of his victims, if he's had any within the last how many hours she has carefully kept track of. He has no nocturnal cravings. He suffers no agonies of thirst nor just the need to bite and enjoy the life leaking out of his victims' body as if it were a broken egg whose yolk seeped through the crack leaving behind the shell to dry out unobtrusively. Still he does enjoy his victim's blood. Why else would he transport them all the way from some remote Russian corner to Paris? For Sasha? Who else? For himself? He must be refreshed by the lustful liquid. His powers, oh his powers. Vio has no idea how much he enjoyed from her lovemaking. Could he travel out of his body? Could he be better than her? Could the dhampire change a human to dhampir, dhampire and even beyond? He could fly, and he could see through her time and space tunnels, an ability neither humans nor dhampirs have. But could he travel out of his body?

"Vio, why are you so threatened by me?" Lev asks, terminating her "freeze" moment and catching her in his strong arms.

"Lev, who is the vigilante?" seems the right question.

"You are, my love." A commotion is heard from somewhere around. "It's Nijinsky. Sasha has dumped him. I have to go."

"What year are we in?"

"It is 1913. Nijinsky has just returned from Brazil married. I was on the ship. Their wedding witness. Of course, Sasha has cut him loose, and Vatsa has an epileptic attack.

We call it a panic attack. Rumola is quite a forceful lady."

"How? When?" Vio asks and quickly replies. "You have played me. You kept an eye on me, holding me prisoner in these quarters, pretending to be interested in my daughter."

"Our daughter, darling." Lev is ready to leave. He chooses the window and the roofs of Paris. "And I am very much worried about her. Our little Annie. I have changed as she has changed. I am quite fond of her, Mashenka. Please watch over her. I will take care of Vatsa."

Back in Podunk, a rising senior, Annie has settled for the ambiguous role of Rose's protégé and most loyal pupil of Princess Zazou. The summer of 1987 happened to be mild and breezy. Like a catchy Bob Dylan song when he was Joan Baez's double. Annie employs her time getting ready for college.

As a present for her 17th birthday, Rose has her over for an afternoon of music,

a tape of Edith Piaf's hits her husband considers packaging for sale, Pepsi served with salted peanuts and Kent cigarettes. Annie finds smoking a worthy attempt to shorten her life in a cool manner, in case she does not make it out of Podunk, to college in the much-desired Bucharest, the Paris of the east. Smoking Rose's cigarette Annie recalls that her mother has no opinion about her smoking or anything else except moving out of the public housing. Oh, and not kissing boys.

"Tifaru, why can't we move this summer? The ground floor is ready and we can finish the house more easily once we live there," Vio relentlessly badgers him when they accidently meet in the kitchen when Tifaru is so thirsty that talking to his wife seems a risk worth taking.

"I still have to hire someone to check the central heating," Tifaru answers and when that reply is overused he moves to "the plumber keeps missing his appointment," and later to "the parquet is not sufficiently dry, and you know how you hate the creaking in the parquet in this apartment." Annie never thought anybody able to bring her mom into submission, but Tifaru certainly is successfully stalling.

"Oh, Rose, I cannot wait to leave Podunk. You were away for four years."

"I did go to college in Bucharest."

"Why didn't you find a job in the world outside Podunk? I certainly won't come back. I cannot wait for this next year to pass by."

Rose kindly smiles without pointing out the implied insult Annie's words contained for her own situation. Then she hands Annie a hardly used English copy of Mark Twain's Huckleberry Finn and an American dictionary of archaic regionalisms.

"Use this excellent dictionary if you have problems understanding the colloquial language," she adds, "but make sure you do not lose them and return them when done."

That gift was a deal no public library would accept. Annie nods ecstatically. Ownership of imagination is what Annie treasures most. Stuff is for her to use and pass it along. She feels so lucky to have Rose take an interest in her upbringing.

Complimented by Rose's high opinion of her knowledge of English, Annie happily returns home, only to note that like in a Dumas sequel, time has added growth though small changes in her neighbors' lives. Sandy, a college graduate, has moved back into her parents' apartment and works as an accountant in the same textile factory as Tifaru. But she remained a Crazy Eights aficionado. How strange, Annie thinks but keeps going. Kaitlin has graduated from one of the many vocational schools available in the county, and was now working in the same secretarial pool as her mother. She is sitting next to Sandy on the bench. Lauren is still the same know-it-all leader of the pack, shuffling the cards. Mia, Annie's frenemy, is lost outside the G&T program. No one remembers her name. Annie is going to skip the brief pleasantry moment, engrossed in the pleasure Huck Finn will soon bestow upon her. Wishful thinking. Kaitlin screams, "Annie, what's the rush? Look who's leaving the building."

As announced, Dan comes out of the building as glamorous sunshine moving in the stairwell. Gliding down the handrail he sports a big smile and an athletic jump. The girls clap and he bows.

Annie blushes, unsure whether she should hurry home past him or just stay put and let the events unfold themselves. She does not have any expectations, only curiosity. They saw each other at Collin's birthday party not even a fortnight ago, and she is still digesting those events. Annie quibbles and waits.

Just before the school year ended, Cordelia, Collin's girlfriend, followed Annie in the girl's bathroom where Annie sometimes shared a cigarette with other less conventional girls in an attempt to diminish her nerdy label, and handed Annie a written note.

"Annie," it read, "I'm having a small gathering at my place for my 17th birthday. Please I would love if you could come. My place, tonight, any time after 7 PM should be fine." It was signed "Collin." Annie looked at Cordelia who was smiling in her non- intelligent way. Annie restrained herself and did not ask her any questions. Cordelia was well-known to dissemble. Once she told Collin that four and four was five, which embarrassed him but not her. Annie folded the note, thanked Cordelia, and put it in the right packet of her uniform, having noted the two different handwritings in two different shades of blue ink.

At the end of the day, Annie showed it to Gabe on their way home from school.

The three of them, Collin, Gabe and Annie were classmates in the G&T class but did not socialize. Cordelia, despite her blond hair and 5'9" height failed twice to join the G&T club.

"Gabe, what do you make of it?" Annie asked her best and only boy friend.

"I don't know. I was not invited, but then I am not part of Collin's posse." Gabe replied placidly. Gabe was a sweet big blubber of a boy. He used to be the cutest kid on the block with his innocent big brown eyes and his curly blond hair, then he just started to eat too much and engage in athletic activities too little.

"Gabe, please come with me." Annie added.

"As your date?" Gabe inquired and a bit of saliva came out of his mouth.

"No, of course not. You should know that we can only be friends." Annie added and took Gabe's hand. "You are and always be my best friend."

Gabe agreed and they both walked to Collin's apartment situated in a fancier public housing downtown Podunk near the park. They climbed up the clean stairs and had no problem locating his place. Dance music was coming out of his apartment. They rang his door bell at 7:15. Within seconds, Collin's dad opened the door. They had seen his face in the local newspaper. He was the head surgeon at the local hospital. He was even more attractive and buff in person, Annie noticed, startled by her own observation. He was wearing a tight pair of jeans and a half buttoned white linen shirt. Behind his shoulder Annie could get a glimpse of a badly lit living room.

"Oh, you brought Gabe with you," Collin's dad observed.

"Yes, Dr. Preda. I did. Are we the first to arrive?" Annie asked staying put outside the doorway.

"Where are my manners? Please do come in. Collin and Cordelia are in his room." He moved making space for them to get by and continued, "I was making some sandwiches in the kitchen, and I should let them know you two are here." Annie and Gabe finally entered.

"Who else is coming?" Gabe asked.

"Oh, I don't know. It's not my party." Dr. Preda added and showed them the way in. They followed him, unsure of their moves. There was a sofa and a small table with a few tea-sandwiches and a bottle of champagne with two glasses, one half full. The floor was emptied as if for dancing. The music coming out of the speakers was a ballad of sorts. Dr. Preda took another sip of champagne and turned to Annie:

"Care to dance?" he invited her nonchalantly and his look, while admiring was making Annie deeply uncomfortable. Annie blushed, unfamiliar with an older man's attention and looked down at herself because she wondered whether she was responsible for this unwanted attention. Her linen dress was see-through in that light and long legs looked even longer now that she was finally wearing the red stiletto shoes Rose sold her.

She turned away from Dr. Preda, and held out her hand to Gabe unsure whether she wanted to dance or run outside with him. Auspiciously, the song ended. In that brief moment of silence, they all heard noise outside the door. The doorbell rang. No one seemed intent on opening the door. Then Dan's voice came through.

"Hello, anybody home?"

Dr. Preda, a good friend of Dan's father, finally went to the door and opened it. "Hello reveler. I guess we are going to have a party after all. Come in, Annie and Gabe are here, too."

Dan, sporting a cigarette in his mouth, went in wobbling and for a moment did not seem to notice anything. He was trying to steady himself. Dr. Preda was moving sinuously towards Annie, when Dan recovered his feline moves, and jumped ahead of him, grabbed Annie's hand and verbalized his motion, "Ready to dance?"

"Ah, so that's how it is done," Dr. Preda congratulated Dan though his approval contained palpable displeasure at Dan's interference. Showing enough self- control, he refrained from uttering any other words. During that verbal duel, Annie freed herself from Dan's grip and moved towards the door as fast as she possibly could without running.

Nicholas told her that when dogs barked you just retreated without showing your fear, because if she went to their jugular those left alive could testify against her in the court of public opinion and she might be driven away or harmed. A life on the run was hard to endure.

She was experiencing emotions she never knew she had. Her heart was really beating as fast as she could take it. A nod was going up her throat, and her eyes, she knew that if anybody saw her in that moment they would see her eyes glowing like a disco ball. Whatever was bottling up inside her she was afraid of unleashing. She needed to escape fast. Luckily, pearls of sweat were forming on her face and she could easily blame the heat. Her hands were shaking and she seemed unable to open the door. She dreaded discovering it locked. She dreaded that she had to push through the locked door to get out. Appearing next to her, Dan bent his head and kissed her forehead sweat. If people would just learn to leave her alone, Annie thought but not for long. Her roller-coaster night was just taking a turn.

"Tasty," Dan said. "Let's go for a walk and a smoke." He opened the door with ease and pulled Annie out the door behind him.

"Are you okay, Annie?" Gabe asked following them down the stairs. She nodded still looking down afraid that her electrocuted eyes would force Gabe to stick around. "Dan, can you bring her home?" Gabe asked not being able to get any useful clues from Annie's measured behavior.

"I don't know if I can do that in my advanced state of inebriation, but I'm sure Annie can walk home now that's she's outside and no one will lock her in again. What do you say, Annie?" Annie nodded again. Dan, who had not talked to her in ages, was helping her escape something she could not yet understand and describe. Dan finally let her hand go. Annie shivered. She was cold.

"Okay. Annie, I'm going home then." Annie nodded again. Gabe walked away.

Watching Gabe depart Dan lit a Kent cigarette. "My dad receives them as gift from the living relatives of those whose bodies he embalms. He does not smoke," and stopped to inhale the poison. "He gives them to me and mom. Watching us get cancer, I guess, despite the fact that we cannot get it," he added with a smirk. Annie was standing next to him watching Gabe disappear inside the park. She wished she went for a walk in the park. "But that's not here nor there." He continued, "sharing the wealth. Care for one?" Annie nodded. A cigarette would calm her down and she would be able to interact with Dan as any normal girl would do, adoringly.

"Annie, tonight was supposed to be your big night." Annie finally looked at Dan. It was her big night. They were talking. She could not remember when they last talked. Dan continued "Dr. Preda won your virginity at poker on Monday. It was all in good fun. Your dad…," then he stopped because the identifier did not seem to make sense next to the rest of his sentence, and corrected himself, "Tifaru had three chances to win it back, but he lost it again, and again, until he also lost the right to go to the police and file a complaint in case you went home accusing Dr. Preda of…".

Dan seemed unable to finish his sentence. Annie noticed he was drunk, but in a different way than Tifaru. When Tifaru got drunk he went to bed. He could not talk or stand up. "…rape." Dan finally added. "But it would not have been rape. The bet was also for Dr. Preda making it in such a way that you would have liked it." Dan did not want to stop. "Very much."

Annie turned away from Dan. She looked up at the sky.

There were no stars. Or she could not see them. In June the days were really long, but she could see the full moon rising up the sky. Annie tried to remember if she read the Almanac that morning. Remembering facts was so reassuring. It helped her stay in control. Stay cool. She could not recall the exact time of that day's sunrise and sunset. She could not recollect the date either. Ah, the school ended. June 15. She felt relieved. Oh, no, she forgot how to conjugate amare, too. Such an easy verb. Her head started to ache, or maybe something else hurt. Dan continued:

"The complaint would not have been really filed anyway, because the local police commissioner was supposed to have you next," Dan added and stopped. He then approached her and whispered conspiratorially: "You are in demand, dear girl, and you have no idea."

He burped, and excused himself. Annie looked at his face. She noticed clogged blood around his right nostril.

"Dan, are you okay?" Annie asked having ignored most of his speech. She was content that she could talk. She thought she was again in control and let herself be fascinated by his big face seen up-close. He was so smooth. His eyes were as big as hers. They had identical eyelashes. She would have liked to close his eyes and caress those velvet-like eyelids and then kiss them tenderly. Kiss. She was getting ready for her kiss. She could hear Elvis Presley's voice:

Love me tender,
Love me sweet,
Never let me go.
You have made my life complete,
And I love you so.

***

"Silly Putty, the kiss," and suddenly Annie was hearing the cello and the harp and the violin in Rimsky –Korsakov's Scheherazade. Annie was Dan's Scheherazade, almost naked rolling in a large very large bed and covered in silk-made sheets. "That's my girl," a voice, other than her mom's, made itself audible in Annie's mind. "That's safe."

"You cannot be interested in my state of being." Dan interrupted her dreaming. "Did you hear what I told you?"

Annie nodded. Dan was right. She could not comprehend anything he was saying. Anyway, it sounded made up by Dan in his drunken stupor. Tifaru liked her. She was a good daughter. He was proud of her. Dan must be confused. But then, Dr. Preda did act in a weird way...

"I'm as drunk as you can imagine," Dan interrupted her train of thoughts this time. Lighting up another cigarette, he continued, "It is possible that this is my last pack." He inhaled and stopped as if to check his digestive system. "Annie, I might be in trouble once Preda calls dad to complain I have interfered with their game of poker," Dan added and stopped. His stomach's convulsions were now apparent. Annie moved closer to him rather than farther away.

"You are not feeling well," she noticed aloud his alcohol induced illness and tenderly touched his arm. He was wearing only a short sleeve T. He felt cold. Straightening up, Dan looked at her and smiled.

"You really love me." He gently took her chin in his hand as if to take a better look at her face. "I like that very much. You must know that I tell everybody how crazy you are about me. We don't even know each other. I surely don't know you. I mean I know you are fucking smart and spend all your time learning as if there was anything worth learning…" He was right, Annie thought. They did not know each other. She was infatuated with him. She had always been since she first saw him in kindergarten. She wanted him. She did not know why or how only that her desires were strong and clear. Annie looked at him. He was a very attractive young man. And more. Suddenly, Annie was afraid. A clear feeling of fear was creeping inside her.

"You are taking it quite well," Dan admired her composure putting out his cigarette. Annie looked at him and touched his hand. Dan was shaking. She was shaking too. She had to run. Instead, he bent and she touched his ear. She stopped her desire to bite it by whispering in it:

"Interfering with some old man's plan to deflower a high school underage girl who's nothing to you was very chivalrous." Annie said admiring her large vocabulary and being embarrassed at the enormous amount of feelings and desires accumulating inside her. She did not know how to handle them. She added as coldly as she could, "Thank you." She smiled and crossed the street going inside the public commons.

The park was alluring. It was the remnants of a small forest which the town had trimmed down and covered with a few pebble-paved alleys and benches. It did not really end. You could go to the river if you walked in the right direction. If anything, unpredictable happened, Annie could go and wash herself before making it back to the public housing. She finally understood why her mother wanted to move out of it so badly.

She did sound so formal and well- adjusted that Dan followed her and finally noticed her. She was not bad-looking. He could consider sleeping with her despite his nagging feeling that he should not touch her. She was a girl he could consider sleeping with. From behind he could see her long wavy hair. She was slim, and straight, and with a determination to do, what, only she knew.

"Hey, so you know how to run. You should join the track team." Dan mocked her in a brotherly way. "You always look as if you're ready to cry when I'm around." He lit his lighter. "But tonight, there was a reason. I got it. Brave girl."

Not even inches apart, Dan gently moved her face nearer. Electricity shot through Annie's body.

"It'll be okay," he whispered sensing her tremor.

"Collin's father wanted to sleep with me, his son's classmate" Annie finally said. "I knew I should not have come there tonight. I don't need to know this town's creeps. I'm getting outahere as fast as I can." Annie talked without turning, until she spotted a clearing with poplars around and a bench in the middle. She stopped and leaned against one of the old poplars.

"Hey," Dan said coming next to her and putting out his cigarette. His voice could have been soothing if it did not invite Annie's tendency to tumult. He gently moved her head toward his. He finally saw her eyes in the moonlight. Electricity shot through Annie's body. "It'll be okay," he whispered. She noticed a small scar on Dan's neck and her Vio's voice sounded in her ears, "Get away, Annie. This is not safe."

Dan, rather unexpectedly said, "I think I always liked your determination to be whoever the hell you are." And he lit another cigarette.

Annie recovered her own self composure and almost shouted "My virginity?" and did a curtsey and giggled remembering her latest literary obsession with Charles Baudelaire, and more than his poetry, his lifestyle and lately, his Belgium lectures. The poet started his second lecture by admitting that he was a novice orator, and he found that his oratorical virginity was as difficult to lose as any virginity, with an equal little or no reason to bemoan their loss. At that time Annie's answer to life was getting rid of her virginity, and ignorance in any form. "My virginity?" Annie added fascinated by the unexpected connection between her readings and her life.

"I don't think they meant it in a bad way." Dan, happy to notice his head stopped thumping. Misinterpreting Annie's obsessive repetition of the word virginity, he tried to excuse his family friend, "You saw, Preda invited you at his home. He had champagne and music for you, and he usually pays very well," Dan stopped. He's been drunk many times, but only now his stomach was going push back its contents. He did not notice the revulsion appearing on Annie's face having realized what her Podunk role was meant to be, the attraction of the summer of 1984. Her acute desire to leave her hometown pit was only intensifying.

Perhaps to stop his stomach, Dan kept moving his lips. "Annie, did you know that dad deflowered my girlfriend, Debby, and you know why?" Annie was waiting politely for him to take a break so she could say good-bye and leave. She was wrong. All her life she had been wrong.

For so many years all she dreamed about was to feel his lips on hers. But she could not do it. Her grandfather warned her just before he died in the car crash she should resist the impulse. "All it takes is a first kiss," he added before closing his eyes for eternity. Just as the longing became unbearable, and Annie's memories were racing back to the questions she had but never dared to pose, "but grandpa, what would happen if I kiss someone?" or even worse, "what if all I want is to kiss one boy, and no one else?'"

Dan was babbling, as far as Annie was concerned, "because the mayor, Debby's dad wanted an older man he trusted to start her." Dan stopped to let the liquor he had generously ingested come out of his body. When done, he continued, "And she liked it very much. She told me that when we had a fight and she was as drunk as I was. Can you imagine that Annie? Now I know why I have had no desire to kiss Debby?" Annie started walking away, "No, of course you cannot imagine the meaning of what I am saying. You are not part of Debby's and my world. Do you know what mom calls you?" He stopped to breathe and light still another cigarette. Annie had stopped counting. "Please don't say anything. Let's forget about tonight," Annie pleaded with him.

He sounded furious. "No, you need to know so you know who I am. Mom calls you Annie T for trash. Annie Trash. And do you know why I came to Preda tonight? Because Debbie dared me. She dared me to do something about it." Dan followed Annie and caught her by her shoulders and faced her. She stopped and stared at him.

Dan's lips met Annie's. The warmth of his mouth sent a current running through her body. Annie threw her arms around Dan's neck as she lost herself in his Johnny Walker breath and soft lips.

And just like that she felt the taste of blood. She did not know whose blood that was, because the change surprised them both. His eyes looked electrifying. And his teeth suddenly elongated were bloody. The kiss could have been over in seconds with either one of them devouring the other. It was not. They somehow realized that it was one of those real kisses few could experience. The world stood still. They both enjoyed the warm salty liquid bonding them in such intimate ultimate manner that they both started to wonder whether they would be able to stay separate or whether they would become one. Dan was the most shocked by this. Maybe because he never thought it possible for anybody, and especially for people like them with such opposite backgrounds. The lack of further blood stopped Dan's adolescent stupor and he suddenly became aware of his surroundings.

"Uh…I have to go," he said stepping back to create space between him and Annie. "I don't want to be late. My parents always wait to have dinner with me."

"Of course," Annie almost smirked. Turning on his heels, he practically sprinted out of the park.

And now, seeing Dan coming out of her building, sober, Annie stops. She feels a sudden pain in her forehead, a cold sensation, a spasm right behind the bone. Dan stops for a moment to let the girls admire his well-built young body. He takes a Marlboro cigarette out of his breast pocket. He turns his head briskly to shake his wavy dark hair, and when probably satisfied with the effect, sits still, lights his lighter, and putting his cigarette between his sensual lips, lights it too. Still avoiding making eye contact with any of them, he approaches them, and for a moment, Annie's full of hope. He will come to her. Cautiously, she moves a step away as if to make space for him to join them without having to be too obvious. Her coolness must have impressed the girls, because when Dan unexpectedly passes by Annie, ignores Mia and approaches Sandy, pulling her towards him and giving her a smoldering kiss, everybody looks at Annie with a gaze approaching moral support.

But it is too late to stop the events. She feels betrayed, and angry, and Damn you, Dan. You don't know who you are playing with my dearest, and that's bad. For you. Out of her a power is growing and a tongue, an immense tongue comes out of her and penetrates Dan, his bones, his veins, his whole being, and he finally explodes. Nothing remains behind except his cigarette. It happened so fast the girls have no time to notice. Annie bends and picks up his cigarette and elegantly puts it out and then into a public garbage bin.

"Hey, Annie, how are you? You look pale." Kaitlyn adds and Annie nods. "You look sick. Go home." Then she turns toward the others. "Wasn't Dan supposed to come out by now?"

"Mom," Annie wakes up from her memory call and screams for Vio through her time loop. Vio is stupefied. Afraid. Scared out of her mind as she has never been before. She saw what Annie saw, but it was not the truth. Anger becomes herself. And shouts.

"Lev, what did you do back then? Are you trying to destroy my child, you bastard?"

***

13 STIRRING THE POT

"Do you know all I wanted to be was a ballerina?"

"Yes."

"I don't know how it came into me. I just had these moments when everything started like a blur through a tunnel. I was not a train stuck in a tunnel. Just a blur zoning out into a daze, then trapped into my mind and music became everything. And out of that blur I would start become aware of my surroundings. First vaguely and then acutely. And do you know what I would see?"

"No."

"I would see myself as Pavlova dancing 'The Dying Swan.'"

"Ambitious."

"Not really. I am a dying Pavlova in 'The Dying Swan.' I had the vision of her dying in 1931 back in 1922 when I was only 3 or so and learning to dream about ballet. I woke up in terror. My breathing was becoming fainter and fainter. It was midnight when I opened my eyes. I tried to make the sign of the cross, but I felt paralyzed. I tried to call mom, Miriam, but my mouth would not move. I started telling my hand to move, but my hand would not move. When it finally moved I had stopped wanting it to move. I had not control over it. I then started thinking that I could make mom wake up and come up to me. I concentrated on waking the animals up so when the cows would moo and the horses would neigh and the pigs would squeal and grunt mom would wake up. The animals started all this ruckus and Miriam still would not wake up. I had Saint-Saens' s Swan be played on the gramophone and ordered myself to get dressed in Pavolva's Swan costume and I started dancing. I was three perhaps, dancing in Pavlova's costume before Fokine choreographed the dance, before she learned how to dance it. It was her dying moment I was choreographing in Radeş, as a 3-year old kid, and do you know who saw me?"

"No."

"Nicholas saw me."

"I was scared but I could not stop either the music or the dance."

"He came close to me and ordered me, 'Now, Maria, you stop this shit and you go back to sleep, before your mama sees this nonsense.' And I did as he told me and I put myself back in bed. I flew into my bed and he walked right next to me and caressed my forehead and said, "You're a good kid, Maria. Now go to bed and forget it all.' And I did right until this moment. Lev?"

"Yes, Mashenka?" "Did you kill Dan?"

"No, Mashenka. That was your daughter. She was in a trance. I cannot say whether she willed herself into that trance, or what, but your Annie has tremendous powers."

"She does not know it. She's been watching her life as a movie. She's neither thinking, nor directing it, I fear. She's just a witness. A second-row witness, the second time around."

"She's up. Let's be quiet."

Annie is up in her office. Voices can be heard through the thick window panels; unpredictable spring and summers keeps people mostly inside behind thick doors. Annie peaks through the blinds tentatively. She catches herself admiring the campus layout with its combination of red bricks and green leaves and grass. All, bushes, flowers, trees, all are still much alive. For a moment Annie closes her eyes trying to see if she can smell their succulent presence. Pleased with the result, she reopens them to follow a young couple laughingly avoiding the raising heat by running from shade to shade and aiming perhaps for the closest AC escape that came with any building on campus. Their intimacy inflames her instinct for self-preservation. They are making space for the other within the available tree-shade welcoming the other's sweaty, naked body parts. His arms are so well defined under the smooth black skin, that her ivory chin reaching for comfort only arouses Annie's imagination. His masculine hand guides her narrow shoulders to the next refuge. They both move fast and erect touched but not intimidated by the apparently approaching noon heat wave. Annie catches the gist of their discussion: they are vacating one sublet for another. She easily assumes they are summer exchange students.

"So, did you find what you needed in your Podunk slumming?" Miriam's voice interrupts her exploits.

"I feel heavy with expectations rather than success. I don't know grandma."

"That was all there was, Annie, time often resemble a fart no matter what others would say."

"You know grandma, you're right. Sometimes my entire life has the smell of a giant fart."

"I use vulgarity because it is devoid of double meaning. But now, you, kiddo, are confusing me." Annie smiles quietly absorbed by the world outside. "Come on, Annie, do your work, and then leave the corporate New York behind and go to Paris. Even I, the peasant vampire from Radeş, Romania, love Paris," her grandmother scores.

"I hear you, grandma," Annie whispers and sits on the windowsill. She keeps tabs on the couple and participates in the conversation with her grandmother, though in a noncommittal way. The kissing stops and she senses the slight discomfort the sublet conversation has brought in. She suddenly longs for that type of disquieting chatter about living needs. That little nothing separates the humans from the likes of her. She has no material worries. She can do as she pleases. One day she reads the Paris Review and submits her short story and the next day her whimsical work gets published to raving reviews. And one is so much more daring than the other that Annie soon discovers she has an "original, alternative" voice. "The voice of knowledge," she would have noted, but the critics always know better, so her voice becomes that of fantasy, so it has to be her imaginative genius, the critics all agree, and soon Annie lives off one academic generosity after the other. The Council quietly approves of her writing proclivity.

She is no vampire vigilante, and procreation does not seem to attract her either, so becoming part and parcel of vampire intelligentsia or better said, its propaganda, saves her future. Intellectual and otherwise.

"Annie, what is going on?" Vio makes herself heard.

"Mom, do you have a moment to spare with me?"

"Annie, why are you hostile to me?"

"I'm not hostile, just surprised that you found time to say hello."

"Annie, I have been around since you've started this memory walk nonsense. Please stop it and start living."

"Funny to hear you preach about living when you're stuck in some era that took place before your own birthday."

"Annie, vampires travel wherever their fancy brings them."

"Only, you and grandma. I am no vampire."

"No, darling. I saw you in action. You are as much of a vampire as any of us."

"You saw me in action? What was I acting in?"

"Oh, kiddo, that's semantics."

"What is semantics, grandma?"

"Never mind, kiddo."

Annie nods and keeps staring outside her window. She is testing her smelling. She sees a young man biting into a cellophane- wrapped sandwich.

"Annie, do you want us to meet in Podunk? You don't have to visit me in Paris, if you'd rather choose Podunk.

Remember, I keep my Podunk residence because I like my neighbors' nosy attention. When they do not see me in the garden they call wondering about my health and whether I would like them to bring me some chicken noodle soup. Thankfully I can answer the calls from Paris. Can you imagine? They fear I may die and they check on me." Vio chuckles.

Annie nods distracted.

"That may be interested, mom. Especially that I think I am almost done with Podunk. Just a few more ends I need to connect."

Annie cannot smell the sandwich and goes back to her seat. If she sits down her memories will call her back to the summer of 1988, the summer when she graduated from Podunk's high school with honors and just learned she made it on the Entrance List. She passed the college Entrance exam, and her name, "Annie Tifaru," topped the list of admitted students.

"Yes, you exceeded all expectations."

"I was the first from the first try," Anny clarifies Miriam's statement.

"Kiddo, yes. No human being could have learned by rote two decades of the President's speeches and two manuals of Marxist Philosophy and Political Economy."

Annie closes her eyes tired. She is back in Podunk, the day the Entrance List made the local news. Tifaru's daughter, yes, the gossip went, the queer's daughter, Annie, passed the law school entrance exam at the top of her entry class. "Do queers have daughters?" was the inevitable follow- up question. "That foxy wife of his, that Violet or something like that, somehow did it."

Tifaru gets off the bus in the center of Podunk, and the congratulations start as he politely elbows his way out of the crowded bus, so he can proudly take a longer walk home. And they cross paths. She is licking a vanilla ice cream cone, chatting with Gabe who is drinking cold Pepsi out of a glass bottle. They are coming out of the town's pastry shop. Gabe is happy too, as he has passed the college exam at his chosen

School of Applied Math and Physics. They do not expect to run into any adults working in the surrounding factories at that in- between-shifts hour. It takes them by surprise to see Tifaru with tears of happiness crawling down his cheeks all puffed up by two much alcohol and sleepless nights. Exchanging furtive scared glances Annie and Gabe seem to suddenly become aware of life's ravenous side effects: too much alcohol makes an adult as sensitive as a child. They both freeze when they see Tifaru crying from happiness. Luckily they cross paths near a street corner and the moment the traffic light changes and the cars stop in mid motion, Annie rushes over the other sidewalk, screaming "I will go to the movies tonight, please tell mom," and turning toward Gabe, she gives him a most luminous smile. She has a splendid fair complexion, lustful red lips, beautiful white teeth and dimples and long wavy strawberry blond hair, quite a rarity. It comes as a surprise to see herself so attractive, yet so insecure.

"Why did you run? Were you ashamed of Tifaru's display of emotion?" Vio asks to make small chat.

"I never thought about him. I just did not feel comfortable with all that gushing and solicitous insincere attention Podunk residents suddenly were bestowing on me," Annie explains herself. "I tried to play fair and learn the hard way. I was as pleasantly surprised as they were about my success, but having been ignored all my life as Tifaru's daughter, it seemed strange to be acclaimed for the same reason."

"How remarkably humble of you, Annie! By the way, why are you fooling yourself? You must know that your brain never told itself to work only at its human capacity. You've always had a head start over your Podunk friends."

Perhaps she knew it. Or perhaps she was experiencing the eternal desire to have your cake and eat it too: a human with extraordinary abilities. While talking to her mom she almost loses track of her memory. Gabe, hurrying to cross the street to reach her almost collides with a car in his attempt to catch up with her on the opposite side walk.

Though speeding way past the legal limit of 40 miles/hour, Annie has recognized the only Mercedes in Podunk. Dan's dad is rushing out of Podunk's pool of unmatched ambition. The morgue director has to face unmitigated shame: his son has disappeared only weeks before the College Entrance Exam.

"You were very happy that entire summer." Vio fast interferes perhaps in an attempt to stop Annie's thought about Dan's disappearance. "You continued to be content with life in the fall too," Vio pushes forward. "You were so ecstatic to move out of Podunk and go to Bucharest and shine like the star you were."

"Don't you find it strange that I want to relive every moment of glory as if I were recapping my life? The fallen angel, from desired to cast out."

"I don't know kiddo. You have so much to be proud of."

"You were going to attend the best university in Romania, and the most coveted faculty in that university, the law school, was going to be your academic playground."

"Yes. For the first time ever, my life seemed perfect."

"Annie, I am a bit uncomfortable. Can we move on? For a vampire of your caliber this small change is disturbing."

"Why? I am bound to have the dreams of my time and place. In that summer my big dreams were hatching possibilities. In the fall I started unfolding my wings."

"Kiddo, from the age of 3 through 10, I saw you every summer for three long months. You were as inoffensive as a light burp, which passed unheard and unsmelled.

I'm happy you found a vocation, writing, because everybody should have a vocation."

"I know where you're going grandma. You think I am not made for big dreams. Big dreams come with big risks." Annie is searching the Internet. A picture of a beautiful blond woman occupies the screen. "I wanted to be like Sylvie Vartan."

"Like whom?"

"Oh, grandma, by 14, I dreamed about having stadiums

filled with people adoring me."

Vio started coughing and Miriam laughing. Annie experiences a burning desire to smash their time loops, but she cannot control anybody else's loop except her own.

"Is she French?" Vio's cough ends. "Maybe your mamma can arrange for you to meet your idol, this Sylvie Vartan? By the way, is she real, as in did she really matter? Who's the gal?" "A minor French singer from the 1960s."

"Wow, how propitious, Annie. Feeling connected with what was insignificant the decade you were born. It's remarkable. You could have picked on the Beatles, for instance, but they were too intimidating. To fill stadiums of adoring fans, as if you were a Beatle female. That sounds like a dream to me. How did you learn about Sylvie?"

"I learned French from old Paris Match issues, you know that. Princess Zazou, my English tutor, saved all the Paris Match issues which reached her in Podunk. She had so many friends abroad and they all took care of her intellectual needs."

"Miriam, Princess Zazou taught Annie English, French and German."

"Princess Zazou?" Miriam continued. "Vio, wasn't she a notorious dhampir who tried to throw over the Council while all along pretending to be a foreign language tutor in Podunk?"

"What?" Annie asks. "You let me be alone with a fierce dhampir twice a week for over a decade?"

"Three times, kiddo. You were learning three languages. Three times a week in order to keep up appearances. As a dhampire, all you have to do is start thinking in French, for instance, and then write it or speak it fluently. Like Voltaire."

"Mom, leave Annie alone. You know how much she admired her Princess," and turning her attention to Annie, Vio continues, "Annie dearest, I was watching over you all those hours. I would have never left you alone with her. But you needed a role model, and she was Princess Zazou, because she made everybody feel dizzy. So, lovely and so well educated."

"Mom, I am speechless."

"Dearest Annie, we were supposed to be perceived as regular folk. I was playing the less educated elementary school teacher and I could not help you without giving away my cover. Can you please, move along with your story?"

"My story? Mom, this is my life I am trying so hard to make sense of it and the more I try the more I see that indeed, my life seems to be a story you wrote."

"Oh, no. You are all wrong. Indeed, I enabled you to rent a small room in the heart of Bucharest, in Cotroceni, but it was all you deciding what to do as a law school student in Bucharest last century. Do you remember how you invited me every month to stay with you for the weekend? We went to the National Theater, to museums, to the Opera House. I loved it."

"It was hard to compete with you and your Parisian life, but for me Bucharest was the anti-Podunk and it just spoke to something in my soul."

"Its lack of structure and laziness seemed so antithetic to you, Annie. What exactly are you fabricating now?"

"I am trying to recollect and understand. From September '85 until the following May '86, I felt the most alive. I lived every day instead of imagining what if I were ..."

"Sylvie Vartan?" Miriam rudely interrupts.

"Grandma, no. That was a dream I had as a pre-teen. By end of my second decade on earth, all I wanted was knowledge. I wanted to understand myself, and my fellow humans and their history, how their world functioned. I would have liked to expose their bravest to my knowledge, had I discovered it, of how societies started in one way and progressed in the opposite direction only to end up where they started."

"Oh, kiddo. You were so deeply pathetic. I guess you had been left alone in your fantasy."

"My life in Bucharest was no fantasy."

"You lived among butchered copies of some pre-war

Parisian residential neighborhood. Vio, which one?"

"I have a hard time finding which one," Vio reluctantly replies.

"I even had human problems. Forcing myself to live within the money Tifaru gave me from your wages pooled together, I encountered disdain and financial embarrassment. I felt belittled by my poverty, when all I could rent was a room but no privacy." Annie continues ignoring the chatter.

"You could have started your Formative Education in Switzerland and forget about the law school in Bucharest."

"Mom, sorry. You are wrong. I was given that chance much later, when it became obvious I had to disappear somehow."

Vio nods admitting that Annie remembers the facts correctly.

"With the money you and Tifaru gave me I could only afford that ground floor room in an apartment while it was being renovated. Its owners, an elderly couple, had moved for those months with their adult children. The rent they collected illegally from students like me, paid for the renovation. Being their home, they treated us like undesired guests and checked our rooms daily while we were in school. Once day, when I found my dirty underwear on a chair, and not on the floor, where I had threw them the night before, I finally had the proof I was too lazy to seek. It forced me to become neat and organized."

"I bought you the Luis Vuitton trunk, remember? You used it to keep your dirty clothes locked in while waiting to bring them home to Podunk every other Saturday so I could wash it for you."

"There were no laundromats at that time."

"No, there weren't and I was only too happy to have them washed in my state-of-the-art washer dryer."

"I was elated most of the time." "You were starving yourself."

"I loved Cotroceni and its quiet streets paved with elms and beautiful pre-war houses."

"If you don't stop this embellishment I would start feeling like a really bad mother who kept you on stale bread instead of cupcakes."

"Leave the child alone, Marie Antoinette. She loved Cotroceni. Period."

Annie nods smilingly. It is one of the prettier residential neighborhoods. The river Dâmbovița crosses it; both the Opera House and the Law School building are there.

"Oh, and I forgot, the famous library. Kiddo, I checked on you a few times. You

were the eternal bookworm spending all your time in that cathedral of useless knowledge. But you did look happy in your tailored gabardine suit among those open books of Roman law. Vio, who's the father of this bookish child of yours?"

"Grandma, I was content. Knowledge was my ambition, and for a while I had access to everything I wanted. I had found a hidden entrance to the National Academic Library, and discovered the locked shelves with manuscripts everybody thought lost. I translated epistles from Latin and old Slavonic. Everything made sense. I even made a few trips back in history and met our forebear, Vlad the Impaler. Mom, you never told me he was my great, great, great uncle."

"Kiddo, he fathered most of the dhampirs in this geographical area, so there is nothing to brag about. And in your case, he tainted your blood, so here you have it."

"I was truly content during my 19th year."

"Really? So why did you change your life's ambition?" Miriam stops Annie's eulogy. "Was it because everything seemed to come so easily to you that you feared you might end up achieving nothing?"

"Maybe, but I didn't really do anything on purpose. It seems that I just followed some instinct larger than my will, grandma."

"How could you behave like any teenager would? How could you develop late teen anxiety? Wasn't that supposed to have skipped you?" Miriam continues ignoring Annie's reply. "Worse, you started talking about Love."

"I did, but then you should not hold that against me. Look what you did for Love, grandma." Miriam chooses not to answer. "My yearning for love was painfully real. Though, thinking back I mostly smoked filterless cigarettes, and drank Turkish

coffee surrounded by a selective group of law school friends intrigued by provincial naiveté."

" I assume there is something alluring to stand up on coffee bar tables and declaim that you were the Don Quixote of Love."

"Grandma, all I wanted was love, please don't make fun of me." Annie tries stop the memories blushing.

"Really? Then how come you settled for the opposite of love, The F..?"

"Mom," Vio cuts her short.

And mute becomes Annie for a few long moments. Her thoughts stop in midair interrupted by the AC humming. She catches her reflection in the computer screen. Her hair is floating as if dancing. It is chilly enough that she could start working. She enjoys her ivory smooth skin forming goose bumps. Her little percentage of human genes is acting out and her frailty pleases her.

"I could not take the emptiness of unlimited knowledge. I was elated by my privileged position, but then, there is a privilege of being a human, too, and that was slipping away from me. Love, which I yearned to know, was becoming more ephemeral each day. The more I was searching for meaning beyond words, the less accessible I was becoming to my fellow students."

"And you dared to kiss."

"I was ready to, but then, as you all know, I made another wrong choice."

She does not need to add much more. They all know that a mixture of all this confusion or just roaring human hormones and a badly timed meeting brought Annie in Robert's room past her regular evening bedtime. Without any begging, she took off her clothes and asked him in as few words as the Romanian language allowed to free her of vaginal virginity which he almost did, and that would have been a bad and unpleasant idea for the two of them and whomever would have happened to be listening, because Robert's room was a former maid's room on a floor full of students living in former maids' rooms in a prewar building in Cotroceni.

"I'm sorry mom. How could I have done that especially after having discovered the truth?

"Annie, don't beat yourself up."

"How could I expose myself like that?"

"Listen, what's done is done. Here we

are. Nothing happened, and his body has yet to be discovered," Vio adds standing up.

"What about Sandy, what happened to her?"

Robert and his twin, Sandy, lived in an apartment below Annie's. They were both 8 years ahead of her in school. Unlike Sandy, who loved to spend free time with kids and adults alike in the building's courtyard, Robert was as much a recluse as Annie was. He was short and frail, and never really grew too tall. Eventually, he did learn to look people in the eye, once he joined the high school band, and played the best solo guitar in years. Nevertheless, kids would move away when he passed by with his guitar. They all seemed afraid of asking him to teach them how to play.

Annie was not afraid of him and soon accepted his offer to stop by his apartment and listen to music. He had a great vinyl anthology. On breaks from her adolescent brooding, they would spend many hours together. He liked classical music, the Russians, especially Rimsky -Korsakov. He also liked Americans, too, The Carpenters. She mentioned The Who to him. He frowned. He was willing to consider Pink Floyd. Genesis was in full swing on Free Europe Radio. They both agreed on Phil Collins. They also discovered that they collected stamps. He was very somber, and talked very little. She liked that about him because chatting was not something Annie did comfortably.

During their public housing years, they crossed paths

haphazardly on their way to the dumpster carrying daily waste. After furtively seeking to identify the other family's diet for the previous 24-48 hours, they would nod and continue their chore. Every family living in the building had a designated member in charge of bringing the garbage to its place of collection, a big dumpster some hundreds of yards away. Usually, the youngest family member who had no right of appeal was the designated garbage boy or girl. The dumpster always attracted stray cats and dogs, but Annie and Robert never had any problems with them.

When Robert started his college years his remote connection with the public housing further endeared him to Annie. Eventually, his quiet solitude made Annie accept taking long walks with him in the forested hills surrounding Podunk, located on the left bank of the sinuous river Dâmbovița. The few times they walked, they did it for hours and talked only if they had something to say. They protected their physical integrity in a sign of mutual respect. They never touched hands, nor kissed. They were two comrades soldiering though life. Annie liked that, because that summer, after her grandfather's death, she feared she would never have similar company. It came as a total surprise when her mother put a brusque end to their walks.

"Annie, I would like you to stop seeing Robert," Vio told Annie the third night she came late from her walks. Annie and her mother still shared their bedroom. Their beds were separated by a chest of drawers. Their villa was a few more years away.

"I just go for walks with him, you know that."

"I know. I cannot put my finger on it yet, but as a favor to me, please stop seeing him," Vio alerted her daughter about the future without worrying her.

Annie stopped, having felt the same unsettled feeling like her mother perhaps. For the next four years, until their paths crossed in Cotroceni, they had lost touch. That late spring evening in 1989, Robert smiled at her. For the first time. She returned the smile.

"Mom, can you see what I remember?"

"Yes. You were flattered you had been noticed sexually."

"Yes, look at Robert. He stops and turns around and whistles, and I follow him to his building. He takes the elevator and I fly up the stairs and open the elevator door for him. He still smiles while he opens the door to the corner designated as his rented room. And there it happens again. A slight headache in her forehead and the power igniting her jumps out like a tongue and penetrates Robert. At first sight it looks as if their blood is on fire, some combustible liquid uniting them, but only his body evaporates and nothing is left beneath the pile of clothes. Nothing.

"Annie, the way I used to do it was to hide their bones in the Catacombs. I would forget where I had placed them. I have not seen anything like this before."

"The fire had shot through the circuit of his veins, invading the marrow of her bones, causing his body to explode. In seconds he was no more," Lev interferes. "I have seen it done once before. An old vampire, dead and light and crisp, save for the constant pumping of the blood he needed to sustain himself. Annie, you are reminding me of him."

"Lev, not yet. Please. Do not interfere yet. Anyhow, she cannot hear you through my time loop."

"Of course," Lev replies with the sadness of people who have made up their mind for display.

Annie is back in Podunk, where the news that Robert has disappeared still has not been really understood. She is at home with her parents. The first year of law school has just ended. The perfect, A+ student is at home.

It is Sunday, early afternoon. Some families are still at lunch. Others are enjoying their siestas. Vio is cleaning the kitchen table and opens the door; a persistent knock has been heard.

"Please, come in," Vio welcomes a disheveled middle-age woman in. "Tifaru, we have company. Ms. Giant is here. Could you please wake up?" Tifaru, tired from working on the construction site of their future home and of drinking too much in the middle of the day, has a hard time waking up and joining them at the table.

"What's going on?" he mumbles freeing the couch.

"Annie, would you make us some coffee, honey," Vio asks her to leave the room

"Vio, Tifaru, I think you know why I'm here. Robert called me yesterday telling me that he and Annie were going to marry. Now, I feel a bit strange to see Annie without Robert. I called him this morning, but his answering machine said he was out. Did Annie tell you where Robert went?"

Annie hears the conversation through the kitchen window. But instead of feeling terrified by the minute, something inside her hardens. Luckily, Vio senses the rising tension and somehow cuts shorts the visit. Robert's mom soon leaves their apartment slamming the door behind her.

"Poor woman," Lev says.

"Yes, and no," Vio sighs. "While unsure where her son was, she nevertheless spread rumors about Annie having violated the lower bourgeoisie rules of behavior: premarital sex. Gosh, was Annie going to be some nice piece of public use meat, or what? The gossip among males started." Vio has a good laugh imagining what Annie would have done with that gossipmonger had she known its extent.

***

14 THE BLEAK HOUSE

"I remember what happened in Romania in December of 1989," Lev caresses Vio's beautiful marble like naked arm.

"Romania? Isn't that too large a country to care about?"

"You're right. Remind me of Podunk.

That's where life takes place."

"Waiting for Robert to come home and explain what the heck was going on, his mom raised the issue of Annie's potential loss of virginity to the level of a lethal disease breakout which needed fast containment. Neighbors started avoiding us."

"What?"

"Oh, dearest, that's okay. It's so last century. I know."

"It's so medieval."

"Anyway, it forced the issue, and Tifaru made the big announcement. We moved away the following weekend. In their new villa, Annie discovered Tifaru had envisaged two identical apartments one on top of each other. He had re-created an improved public housing for two families: his and Annie's.

Back in her memory loop, Annie sees herself and Vio holding hands with Tifaru in a rare moment of silent contentment. It was a first.

Inside their home was starting to reflect Vio's double

life. She brought in Parisian furniture and had a Persian rug in every room, except the kitchen, which looked very much like her old kitchen for the same of her friends. Luckily they needed that appearance of continuity as much as she thought they did.

The 3000 square ft. ground floor had two bedrooms, one for Tifaru and one for Vio, and an enormous living room with a fire place. The kitchen had its own terrace and a pantry. The bathroom had everything including a bidet, and the stairwell to the floor above had a huge window looking out an old vineyard which came with the half acre of land. The apartment upstairs had the same layout. Annie chose her bedroom above the kitchen. She like that space, because it faced the backyard, instead of the street.

Annie refused to use the bedroom with a view of the street. She could look straight into the bedroom once occupied by her now defunct tutor and mentor, Princess Zazou. There had been two years since her Princess decided to join her family somewhere out of anybody's reach, but Annie was still mourning her loss.

"What happened to Zazou?" Lev inquires.

"No one really knows. It is possible that she finally moved in with her lover, the writer, but because they both had human histories they had to put on a nice death before they could reunite," Vio explains.

Back watching Annie's memory, they witness her recollection of Zazou and Annie's history. Annie recalls her year of pain when Dr. Lucien ignominiously submitted to a national competition a poem by the Roman poet Catullus, as being hers. She shared her fears with the Princess, who encouraged her to wait and develop the strength to face the music if necessary. As always her princess understood her conundrum, and her advice was always devoid of the predictable schadenfreude. Dr. Lucien, a close friend of Bacchus like so many in Podunk, drowned in the river when the dam was opened by mistake and everything disappeared with him as if it never existed.

"But that is not what really happened, is it?" Lev asks an

unresponsive Vio.

She is taken by Annie's memories. Annie had found The Broken Rode by Patrick Leigh Fermor, infamously published in Greek in the 1980s, among the pile of readings the Princess let her choose from. Annie saw a picture of the author with a young woman looking strikingly like a picture of Zazou young, which was hanging in her attic apartment. Annie was determined to ask her if she was his love. Annie was ready to ask her princess if she was originally from Băleni, near Galați, and that childishly prosecutorial attitude perhaps forced Zazou's decision.

"Did you actually talk to her or you just showed up holding the book in an accusatorily manner?" Vio calls to her daughter.

"Mom, why are you accusing me of shortening her life?"

"No, my dearest. You helped her get out of a very sad façade of a life and reunite with her love. Your hunch was correct. She was his only love."

"I miss her."

"I'm sure she liked you a lot too." Annie moves back in her memory to 1987, when Zazou disappeared. It's the day of French, or English, or Russian. She keeps re-reading pages from the Broken Rode while walking. Still reading she opens the gate, almost trips, and then ashamed at her clumsiness she closes the book and runs directly to the rope attached to the bell, which anybody rings to alert the princess someone is looking for her. Annie pulls the rope once, twice and continues to do so stubbornly and childishly, refusing to leave until her princess's landlady, a distinguished widower all in black not much older than her princess, comes out all teary, telling her that the princess passed away.

"Who gets cold in July?" Annie asks. "And who dies of a cold?"

"She collapsed at noon," the landlady continues, "I called the doctor. But it was too late." The woman is crying and Annie knows that she is supposed to hug her. She cannot. She has never spoken to that woman before in her life. "We will bring her here tomorrow and we will have her in an open casket for friends to come and say goodbye. She wanted to be buried in the family church on their land in Băleni."

On her way out, Annie touches the lilies her princess planted. So much joy she has had from their blossoms. Looking down and mumbling something polite, Annie rushes out closing the gate behind her firmly but noiselessly, as her princess would have liked. On the sidewalk, Annie feels no direction.

"Annie," she hears her name and from a hundred yards away, Rose is waving to Annie to come to her. Rose used to be tutored by Princess Zazou, too, and she loved her perhaps as much as Annie did.

"Come in, you little kid," Rose welcomes Annie in her arms, open for the first time since she bought the red stilettos. "I guess you heard the bad news. Come in. Let's talk out our pain."

And they talked. Rose told Annie how her parents, high school teachers in Podunk, were the first to notice the Princess and her husband, two well-bread, athletic looking, well dressed middle-age people standing on the platform, each holding a small piece of luggage and the other's hand. Their train ticket was to Podunk, and they were waiting their fate on that empty platform.

Unlike Annie's grandparents, Princess Zazou was regarded as part of Romania's aristocracy. She had endeared herself to the hundreds of peasant working her estate by living there rather than visiting from Paris.

"She had no use for dhampirs to run her business." Annie notes.

"Probably being one of them, she could do the work herself." Miriam comments.

When at the end of 1949 the Romanian state nationalized her domains, she let herself and her then acquired husband, appear homeless, Rose continued her story. With 15 minutes given to pack a small piece of luggage and an escort to the nearest train station, she picked up her ticket and learned her destination, Podunk. More than 24 hours later, the Princess and her husband managed to remain composed and smile at Rose's parents who greeted them with no questions but a suggestion. Not far from their own house, a childless widower was looking for tenants, "Would you like us to take you there and see if you'd consider renting her room?"

The Princess and her husband liked the separate entrance and the isolation of the attic. They occupied the entire third floor. Her husband had studied engineering and he was soon hired in a local factory. The Princess started tutoring working class children in French, English and Russian.

"Mashenka, stop sneaking into Annie's walk on memory lane."

"Dearest, we have nothing to do until tonight when we go to the theater and then return her to entertain my ballet friends and watch you interact with Sasha."

"Oh, you're finally admitting you are keeping an eye on me."

"Dear Prince Myshkin, you are wild and unpredictable. I have to." And they giggle like teens and run until they push each other in a bathtub as big as a small swimming pool, when they quietly collapse and let themselves happily float. That could have been the test that none of them is of pure vampire blood.

Annie has moved forward with her recollections. She's back in 1989. The summer of 1989. While having been lonely all her life, Annie, the rising second year law school student, feels unbearable loneliness the day they moved into their new home. She misses her inquisitive public housing neighbors. She misses even more her new university friends. After much tossing and turning she finally falls asleep. That first night in her own bedroom. No nightmares to fend off. Still she wakes up a few times. She decides to heat a glass of milk. She goes downstairs into the kitchen. She enjoys stepping over the soft, thick, lushes, Persian runner covering the cement of the stairs. It's full moon, and its shine makes the leather furniture look alive. Annie shivers with anticipation. At the bottom of the stairs, Tifaru is sitting down on a lazy boy drinking some plum brandy with his eyes closed.

"I'm going to retire this year." He announces. Annie knows it is just the two of them. So, she answers.

"That will be good for you. There is so much work to be done around the house, inside and outside. We could plant a small orchard in the back and flowers in the front," Annie suggests.

"Do you know what they use to threaten me now with?" Tifaru suddenly stands up. Annie looks at him quizzically. "With your future. Even on Friday they called me to their party office and shouted at me, 'Hey, comrade Tifaru, your daughter's future seems all secure. She is so bright. Nothing, or very few things could stop her ascendance.' And I just stood there knowing that they were toying with me. And then when I left I closed the door and stood there for a few minutes. I heard them o on laughing as if they said something really funny."

Annie feels uncomfortable. She does not want to know what this is all about. Her body aches too tired to focus her attention on anything important. "I'm going to heat some milk," she says passing by and going to

the refrigerator. Something in her likes Tifaru. Sometimes she thinks she likes him more than her mother.

"Mashenka, did you hear her thoughts?"

"I did, but how did you hear them?"

"I'm her father. Have you forgotten that small detail?" Lev splashes her. They both become silent as Annie recalls how she used to play chess with Tifaru and discuss Marx's Capital with him.

"They shared happy moment," Lev adds and Vio is unable to read their meaning: jealous or joking.

Annie gets her glass of milk and then joins Tifaru, sitting on the ottoman. "They used to threaten me with Gigi, but now that he's dead." Tifaru stops. Annie cannot not see his face, but his voice is sad. Gigi used to be his best friend. She touches his hand, and then she recalls what Dan told her a while back.

In a bitter sweet moment, she reminisces about her own Battle of Vosges, about the competition among the Podunk soviet aristocracy, the high-end echelon of local informers, for her deflowering.

"Is she going there? Again?"

"What the heck is going on with this girl? What more is to find out there?"

But nothing can stop Annie recalling how it all started during a night of poker where she had been auctioned to the higher bidder.

"I cannot watch that." "Close your eyes."

They do, until Annie's memory ends with her sitting there, at the bottom of the stairs in their own two-story Podunk villa. Annie feels she has lost the battle, despite having played her cards as she wished, with no one dictating to her what to do. How strange how she has chosen to trash something before she could understand whether it had any value to her. It's irremediably lost. She does not know whether she should describe her gesture as stupid, or experimental. And Robert is gone now too. For the better, she thinks and smiles.

"Do you know how I got this piece of land?" Tifaru asks out of the blue. Annie is too preoccupied to answer. She is sure Tifaru's drunk. "I bought it with the money I saved during the years I lived with mom. Before the party sent me to college on scholarship." He sounds hopeful for a moment but then he quickly adds, "only to rescind it and make me abandon my studies."

"You won it at poker." Annie shortens his story while correcting his recollections.

"I never played poker. Never." Annie, baffled and a bit annoyed, stands up.

"It's late. I am going upstairs. You should go to bed too," she sounds maternal.

"I never played poker, Annie. You must believe me."

"We shared a one-bedroom apartment and you were out

most of the time. You played when you were with Gigi, and you continued to play without him. I know you played poker," Annie reminds him.

"No, you know that I was going out those nights. I was the one arranging their games at Gigi's place." Tifaru continues. "Do you remember uncle Gigi's house? It was right near our public housing complex."

"Why?" Annie asks him intrigued.

"They forced me to. They knew about me and Gigi, and that was their blackmail."

"You never played poker?" Tifaru shakes his head in denial. "Not even once with Dr. Preda?" Annie cannot help herself.

"Never. Those were sick people." Tifaru looks down slowing his speech till it reaches silence.

"So, you did not know … about Dr. Preda's intentions regarding me?" Annie uses a euphemism to describe that night.

"I cannot say I did not know because I was there when he and the police commander played poker for the privilege of entrapping you. I could not do anything about it. They would have exposed me and fired me and what would have become of me? I could not have survived the scandal, you must understand that." Tifaru adds.

"Your future was more important than your own…." Anny catches herself and stops.

"Did she believe he was her father?" Lev sounds jealous.

"Daughter would have been the right ending. Maybe it just came to her as a dramatic ending solution," Vio explains drying herself.

Back in Annie's recollection, Tifaru defends his actions, "Preda promised he would not force you to do anything you did not want to do. Nothing. …." Tifaru cannot not finish his sentence either. Judging by his remorse he relives those humiliating moments.

It is too late in the night for any serious talk. "Its fine," Annie finds the strength to end it all caressing his hand. Her forehead though is pulsating and the pain this conversation has caused her is becoming too much for her to contain.

"I'm sorry. I have not been able to help you too much," Tifaru adds, "but now we have our own house to bury our sorrow." Annie smiles at him and almost kisses his skull. Bending though, something else arouses her and more happens. The pain behind her forehead just grows beyond her control. It takes over her mind and powers. It acts out as a deadly embrace. For the first time she realizes she can kill without his body catching on fire. Rather his heart and brain have suffered a kind of rupture.

"Vio she did it again, and she knows she did it."

"Lev, what can we do?"

"It is very simple. She has to come to be with us. We have to keep our eye on her."

"Mom." Annie screams, standing in her New York office. "Mom, open your time loop please. I am coming to you."

"Annie, there is no need for you to come. No need."

And then they all see Miriam and Nicholas dancing in flames, dying, caught in a dance with twisted arms and legs, as Annie is fighting Nicholas with a pitchfork.

"Lev, who brought in this vision?"

"I did it, Vio," Miriam's voice is heard and her time loop opens to New York. "Did you see it, Annie?"

Annie is flying through the time loop to Paris, but her mom stops her.

"Not through my time loop."

"I am going to open mine. I'm coming.

We need to talk. I come in peace."

"We all have heard those menacing words before, 'I come in peace.' Stay away Annie. I cannot promise I will not fight you."

"I'm not coming for you. I'm coming for him."

"For your father?" "And your father too." "What?" Vio exclaims.

"That's Nicholas, or Lev, or whomever he likes to tell you he is." Annie stops for a moment. "Definitely a father. Definitely a fighter, or an instigator. He has controlled my actions for much too long."

***

15 EPILOGUE

"That little dagger is still hanging in." "Hidden in my layers of silk."

"I'm sorry I had to pull this memory call game on you, mom."

"I'm sorrier I had exposed you to all

this."

"We are vampire vigilantes, aren't we mom?"

"You too?" "Grandma too."

Miriam's coughing can be heard. "I may be dead but I am still watching over you, my girls."

"Did you know about Nicholas/Lev, too, mom?"

"No, I don't even know how I died. Annie made us both watch it fast, because she was in a trance too."

"Nicholas, my grandfather and father, called me. I came in time to watch him kill grandma. I was too late to save her. The house was burning and she was held down by a pitchfork. I was ten, remember, but had no problem lifting that pitchfork and impaling him. I had no memory, but having done it, that night became recorded forever."

"You acted like a dhampire before you had the knowledge about your nature."

"And then you rejected it, and forced yourself to be human."

"Talk about repressed memories."

"Nicholas would not let me forget. He enticed me with the kiss. I fell for Dan, a dhampir's son and the likelihood of biting each other was too much for him to ignore."

"All this, while he was lying in bed next to me, pretending to be a human transformed by my love."

"Mom, Nicholas was not a mere vampire. He was a very sick, depraved one, the most dangerous hybrid the Council gave me to watch."

"And I had to watch Lev."

"Actually mom, Lev made you believe that. You have created this eternal Mobius time loop where you are stuck in 1909 because he could keep you under strict surveillance. You thought that he would otherwise die, like Nicholas, a mere human bitten by a dhampir, or as Sasha and Vatsa would. But all he wanted was to make sure you are useless as a vigilante."

"You saved me."

"We all saved each other."

"I really did not remember most of my life. When you choose to repress memories, you cannot really choose which ones to enjoy and which ones to forget. They all get lumped together."

"I've been a bad mother on so many layers."

"You haven't."

"Girls, stop the nonsense. There is so much more work to be done."

"Do we know what happened to Nicholas/Lev?"

"The moment you let the time go by he moved on too. He may come up at any moment."

"As a man?"

"Certainly not a man."

"The gender? Who knows. The Council is unsure about his true nature. He certainly can switch from one destiny to another as if we ran through one-time loop and then switched to another one."

"But we can end him one destiny at a time. I ended his Nicholas deception. He cannot be that ever again."

"But Prince Myshkin?"

"If you bring up that time loop, you may find him somewhere."

"Annie, you did all this for me. I cannot thank you enough."

"I cannot tell what I did for you, for me, for the Council. I had to face my father. You were not going to reveal his identity to me."

"I did not know half as much as you knew."

"They look very much alike, mom.

Nicholas and Lev."

"I never paid attention to Nicholas. He looked like a dirty peasant to me. And then, the trick with the denture, and the old age."

"I know. I was tricked too for a long time, and I was his wife."

"No, grandma. You have been drugged most of the time. I don't know what he used on you, and my assignment was to find that too. I thought I could find out if I revisited my life with you, but I failed."

"Kiddo, you are the best of us."

"I am Nicholas's offspring twice." "Could he have taken over your destiny kiddo?"

***

16 THE LAST (KNOWN) LETTER FROM JM

Dear all,

And that's the last and most I have been able to find out about them, Annie, Vio, and Miriam. For me, an admirer of the late Alexandre Dumas, they will always be the three musketeers, Porthos, Athos and Aramis, trying to find the evil, Cardinal Richelieu, and corner it.

Life is not about winning over the evil, or making sure the good overcomes it. Life is giving everyone a chance. At least that's Dumas thought, and they [sic] knew best.

When Diaghileff stopped biting Nijinsky, Nijinsky stopped being the dancing genius we all knew. He became a choreographer. That prolonged his life, but no one can tell about the happiness he knew during those years. Diaghileff tried to continue his deprived dhampir ways, but dhampirs are not immortal, so eventually he became a story, too.

Prince Myshkin started as a story before Nicholas became Lev. For all I know, and I have not had much time to investigate, his best has been achieved as a story.

Of course, I will continue to find out more about them, and as I do, I will make sure I will let you know.

Until then, fondly,

Jordan Muncz,

(From a café near you)

ABOUT THE AUTHOR

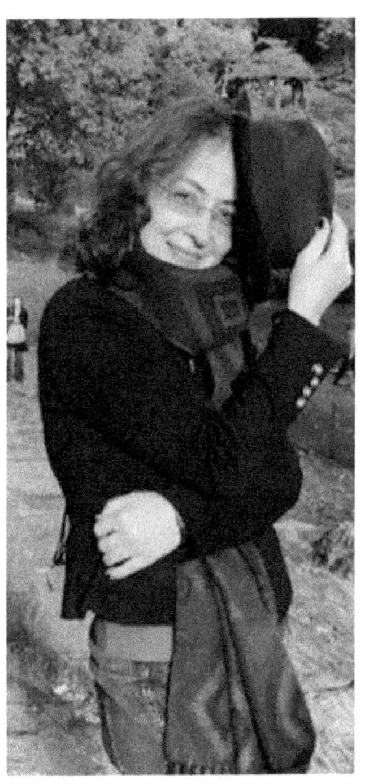

Jordan Muncz is a fearless citizen journalist. She is always on the look for new topics. Sometimes topics find her and then the unthinkable happens. She has to go into hiding, and she will remain there for as long as readers seek her books. The good news is that her publisher knows her whereabouts.

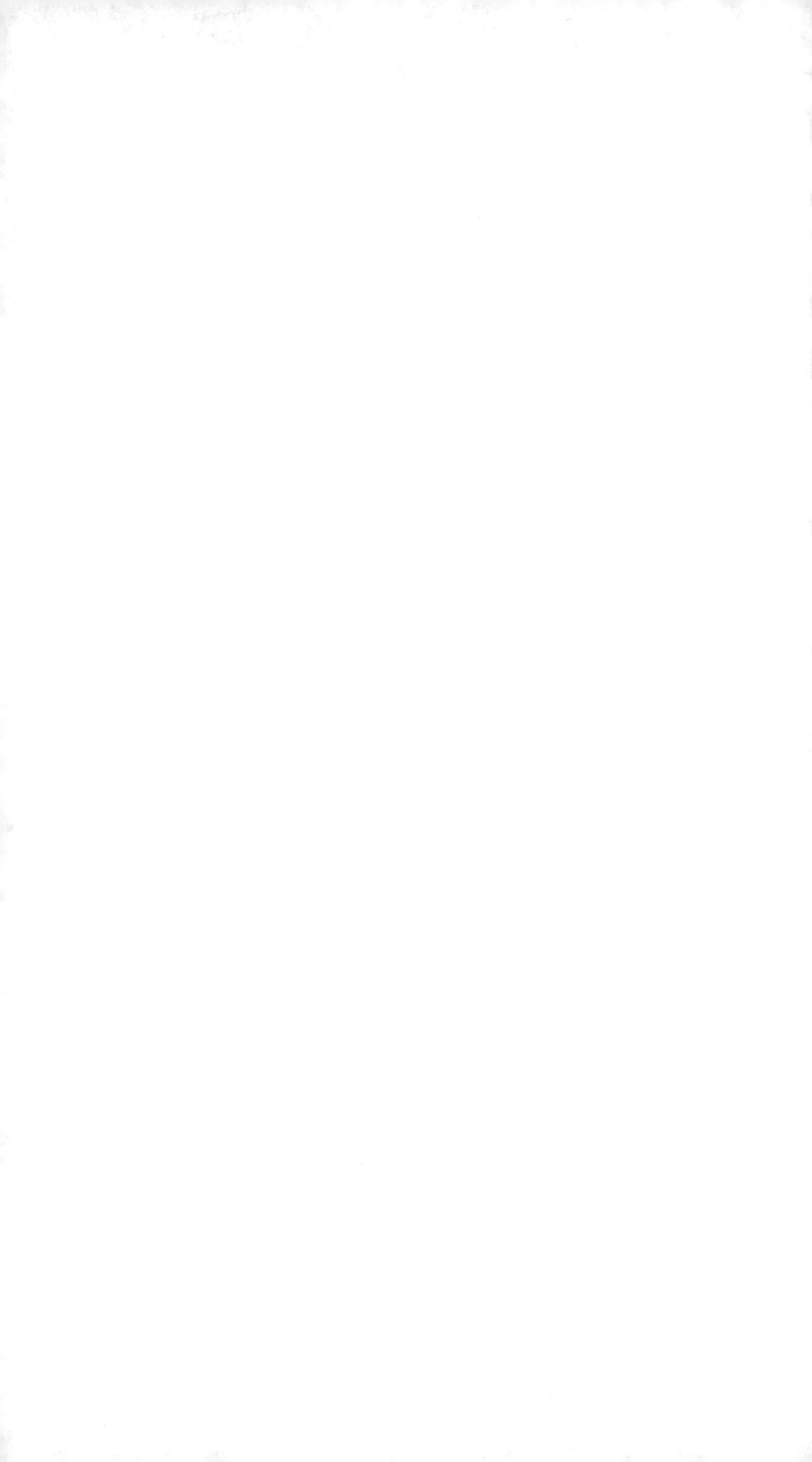

www.ingramcontent.com/pod-product-compliance
Lightning Source LLC
LaVergne TN
LVHW010701110826
845149LV00014B/3187

* 9 7 9 8 9 9 0 7 9 4 0 1 6 *